Carolyn had that eerie [feeling of being] observed, and a cold chill snaked down her back. Her topaz eyes widened at the sight of the tall, lean-waisted, broad-shouldered stranger who leaned languidly against the railing of the little bridge. His dark eyes were fastened on her intently.

She drew in her breath at the sight of him. His black hair, trimmed in a Brutus cut above an angular sardonic face, tanned bronze by a searing sun, frightened her. Yet at the same time she experienced a strange new feeling.

A sudden humorous glint flickered in the man's penetrating eyes. "Ah, Sleeping Beauty," he said, mockingly, "you've cheated me. I was about to play Prince Charming and awaken you with a kiss."

"Sir!" Carol cried. "How dare you speak to me in that degrading manner? I'm not who you may think I am!"

Supposing her to be a barmaid from the inn, he decided to go along with the game.

Unbeknownst to either of them, they had set the wheels of fate in a strange motion. . . .

Second Season

a novel by

Pauline Draper Marrs

FAWCETT COVENTRY • NEW YORK

SECOND SEASON

Published by Fawcett Coventry Books, a unit of CBS Publications, the Consumer Publishing Division of CBS Inc.

Copyright © 1979 by Pauline Draper Marrs

ISBN: 0-449-50012-8

First Fawcett Coventry printing: December 1979

Printed in the United States of America

10 9 8 7 6 5 4 3 2 1

Chapter One

It was an early spring morning, but winter's chill still hung about the drafty rooms and corridors of Worster Hall, thus there was a roaring fire in the book-room wherein sat Raymond, Marquess of Worster. His gouty foot, heavily bandaged, rested on a low stool in front of him, and an expression of pain mingled with anger twisted his usually placid facial features into a deep scowl. Lady Carolyn, his daughter and the recipient of his frown, was seated close by in a straight slatback chair. They had seemingly reached an impasse, and each stared at the licking flames of the fire without actually being aware of it. Lady Carolyn spoke first, rising from the delicate chair and stamping her dainty foot in a most unladylike manner.

"I do not *want* to go to London for another Season and I do not see *why* you insist I do so! You know very well last year was a disaster. I had two offers of marriage. One from Lord Oglesby who was so old he *tottered*, and the other from young Mr. Carraway who eloped with Dolly Foster when he discovered her fortune was bigger than mine and would be at his disposal much sooner." With the speed of a chameleon, her furrowed brow became smooth, her shapely lips curved into a coaxing smile as she knelt beside his chair, her soft hand touching the sleeve of his velvet dressing gown. "Please, Papa, don't make me go. Let me stay here at the Hall, take Mother's place as the distaff head of the family, help Mrs. Bartlett run things, see to the needs of Oliver and Lily."

"Return to your chair, daughter, and listen to what I have to say. Your wheedling ways and beguiling smile will do you no good." He waited until Lady Carolyn was back sitting stiffly in her chair, her lower lip protruding petulantly, angry lines again creasing her fair brow.

"To be sure, you were sorely mistreated by that rascal Carraway, but in the end you benefited by not being tied to an odious fortune-hunter. And as for Lord Oglesby, you know I wouldn't have agreed to let you marry an old fool like him even if you had wanted it." The marquis's scowl faded, a smile formed instead. "Carol, my lovely daughter, I don't want you wasting yourself at Worster Hall, and I don't need you to help Mrs. Bartlett. She has done an excellent job ever since your mother died, God rest her soul, and I'm sure will continue to do so for many years to come. As for you taking care of your brother and sister, that is unnecessary, too. Oliver has one more term at Eton, then it's off to Oxford for him. Lily at fourteen is long out of the nursery, but is still in the schoolroom, and Miss Kindersly takes very good care of her. Edward reached his majority three years ago and since he spends most of the time at his London house, he has no need of your care, either. *But*," he paused, pointed a finger at her, "it's my duty to take care of *you.* And I shall perform that duty in spite of your obstinacy. I intend to spend what few remaining years I have left satisfied that I've done everything Lillian would have wanted me to do had she lived, and seeing that you make a suitable marriage is of prime concern."

His reference to his "few remaining years" stabbed at Lady Carolyn's tender heart as her father calculated it would. When he saw her lower lip quiver slightly, he knew he'd already won the argument, but knowing his daughter, he knew he had a bit further to go before she capitulated completely.

Taking up where he left off before she had a chance to say anything, he said, "I realize what with your great-aunt's inheritance, plus what you will receive from me, that you will be a very wealthy woman when you reach the age of twenty and five, and there's always the chance you will encounter men who are more dazzled by your money than by your charms, but really, Carol, they are in the minority. There are many men of rank and breeding who will want to marry you for yourself alone. Those are the men I want you to meet, and if you bury yourself here in the country, you'll never have any opportunities to meet that kind. Besides, since you desire to be so helpful to your sister, think of the advantage to her if you made a suitable match. As an accepted matron of the *haut ton,* you could see that Lily had the same opportunity." Lord Worster smothered a smile as Carol turned to face him, her stubbornness almost gone from her amber eyes.

Again not giving her a chance to speak, he pressed his point home. "Then, too, my dear daughter, I could not rest comfortably in my grave if I knew you remained a spinster. That's no life for a lady, wealthy *or* poor. I couldn't bear to see your sunny disposition turn sour and your soft melodious voice take on the strident tones of a harpy which I'm much afraid would happen if life passed you by." He lowered his eyes in a manner befitting so dismal a thought, but not before he saw full surrender to his will in hers.

Carol sighed. "All right, Papa, I'll go. I'll try to find a kind man that meets all your requirements so that you can rest comfortably in your grave. I'd hate to be the cause of your twisting and turning throughout all eternity." The irony of her tone wasn't lost on him, and it brought an involuntary smile to his lips. Carol looked over at him at just that instant and she couldn't help but smile, too. Lord Worster reached out a hand to his daughter and caressed her warm fingers with his.

"Thank you, dear. I know you're doing this to please me, but if you'll just try to forget last Season and start over fresh, you might find you will enjoy every minute of your stay in London. After all, you're only nineteen and have several years before you're considered an old maid. But there's one thing I want you to remember. I'd never force you to marry someone against your will. Remember that's my promise."

Her fingers pressed his in return. "I will, Papa, and I thank you for it." She rose, stood with her back to the fire. "I have one more request, Papa. While I'm in London, why can't I stay with Edward instead of Aunt Minnie? It would be ever so much more fun."

8

"Maybe so, but I will not permit it. Edward has an adequate staff of servants for a bachelor, but none I would entrust with your care. As my sister as well as the wealthy relict of Sir Charles Simms, your Aunt Minnie has entrée to every respectable home in England. She is the perfect chaperone for you this year, just as she was last year. However, you can count on your brother as an escort anytime you feel it necessary. You just can't make your abode at his house."

It wasn't in Carol's nature to hold a grudge nor to stay angry for very long, but as she flounced— there was just no other word to describe her ascent up the winding stairway that rose to the third floor—to her bedroom her thoughts were not the sweetest she'd ever had. She knew her father had her best interests at heart and she didn't doubt that he loved her deeply. What she did doubt was her finding the suitable match he wanted for her. On reaching her room, she crossed over to the oval mirror that hung atop her massive dresser, and peered at her reflection. Nothing about her met the *ton*'s standards that ensured a successful Season. For one thing, she thought, she was a shade too tall, with long tapering legs and an erect spine that supported a pair of strong shoulders. Oh, not really *broad* shoulders, but not the thin sloping kind that smaller girls had. She also thought her eyes too wide-set and of such an undecisive color. She was completely unaware that her sherry-colored eyes with their golden flecks and thick fringe of black lashes could melt the heart of the most jaded of swains. She would have been surprised if someone told her that her chestnut hair, which she thought of as just plain brown, was like a cascade of molten bronze as it rippled down her back when she brushed it at night by candlelight. She would have been astonished, too, if anyone had described her classic facial features as akin to Venus's, and compared her smooth skin to the bloom of a May peach. All she could see was a leggy girl with a mop of brown hair over a face tanned by riding in the sun too much. No, she thought to herself, this Season won't be any better than last year, but for Papa's sake, I'll give it a try. Thank God, I can ride well, handle the ribbons of a spirited pair, and can manage to dance well enough to keep my feet off my partners' and theirs off mine. I'll bridle my tongue, agree with everything men say, smile and simper with maidenly modesty, even if it goes against the grain. Even if I gain a fortune-hunter, maybe he'll be respectable enough for Papa, and pleasant enough looking so that I can be submissive to him as a proper wife should.

At that point, she turned from her mirror, walked over to look out the window. From her vantage point, she could see the stables, the meandering stream that flowed by the edge of the woods and the well-manicured gardens below. She was thinking of herself as a wife. Though she'd led a very sheltered life, she was not ignorant. She knew what was expected of a married lady. That was why she hoped whoever she married was not repulsive looking and kept himself clean-smelling. But oh, she thought sighing deeply, if only I could fall in love and be loved in return! The few novels of Miss Austen's pen and those of Frances Burney and Mrs. Radcliffe that she'd read all highly extolled the bliss of a wedded pair. Carol fervently hoped that some-day that kind of love would come to her, but, turn-ing from the window to ring for her abigail, she really didn't have much hope that it would.

Ada, her nurse turned abigail, came into the room, and Carol asked her to lay out her new green riding habit. There was a teasing twinkle in Carol's topaz eyes because she fully expected Ada to get out her old brown habit instead, saying that she should save the new one for London. Though Ada called her "ma'am" and treated her with the defer-ence due the daughter of a marquis, there were times when her tone of voice and pointed glances were more like those of a mother-hen than a maid. But not this time.

Without a word of dissent, she began laying out the new unworn green garment that had just re-cently been completed for the London Season. Her salt and pepper hair was done up in her usual neat bun on top of her head, but her blue eyes, as a rule bright and good-humored, were watery and showed the red-rimmed aftermath of recent tears.

Forgotten was the teasing Carol intended to in-flict on her old nurse-cum-maid cum-friend. She hurried to take Ada's hand, turned her around to face her. "Ada, what's wrong? Are you ill?"

Taking a large handkerchief from her apron pocket, Ada blew her nose, then looking at her mistress, she started to speak. Instead, she burst into tears. After a moment or two, Carol managed to quiet the distraught woman, and in quiet tones asked again what was wrong.

"Oh, ma'am, it's my George. He just can't seem to get well. He coughs night and day, and he's so worn out it's plumb hard on him to draw one breath after the other." Ada dabbed at her eyes, continued, "I've done all I can for him, but nothing seems to work. I'm at my wit's end. And Miss Carol, I—I don't feel right about going off to London with you and leaving him with just the two girls to see to things."

"No, of course not, Ada. You need to stay here and look after him yourself."

Despite her concern for Ada's husband, Carol couldn't help but wonder who would look after her and see to all her clothes while she was at Aunt Minnie's. George Ellis was one of the best grooms Worster Hall ever had, and had been sorely missed during his two months' illness, but there were enough men to carry on the work nicely. But who could take Ada's place?

Ada herself solved that problem. "Ma'am, if you would be willing, Flossie could go with you to London. She's sixteen now and if I do say so myself, has a knack for fixing hair real stylish-like. She's handy with a needle and thread and can iron ruffles and tucks beautifully with nary a scorch place to be seen. And," Ada lowered her eyes, twisted her handkerchief in her work-worn hands, "besides, I'd like her to get away from that Woodson boy. He's dangling after her like a love-sick calf. I'm just not ready for my Flossie to get married yet, especially to the likes of him. I'd like for her to see a little bit of somewhere else beside Worster village afore she settles down."

Carol took Ada's hand into her own, pressed the cold fingers with her warm ones. "I'll be delighted to take Flossie to London with me. I hadn't realized she's grown up so. Seems like only yesterday she was a skinny little girl shyly hanging onto your skirts." She smiled at the memory. "Besides getting her away from an ardent admirer and giving you the chance to nurse George back to health, I think I'll enjoy having a young abigail. At least, I won't be the only person under forty staying at Aunt Minnie's. You send Flossie to the Hall tomorrow and we'll start getting used to one another."

A week later everything was done preparatory for Carol's exodus to London. Flossie was well established into the household staff, and already Carol depended on her completely for suitable arrangements of her long wavy hair. Trunks and bandboxes and bootboxes were packed ready to be loaded into the light carriage which was to follow Aunt Minnie's chaise and four.

Lady Minerva Simms distrusted any vehicle save her own with her reliable coachman handling the reins, so it was no surprise to see Aunt Minnie's chaise drive up the gravel sweep to stop in front of her ancestral home. What did surprise her was to see Lord Lynsford alight first and hand Aunt Minnie out before the footman had a chance.

Running gaily out to meet them, she held out her hand to her brother, crying, "Edward! What a delightful surprise!"

A taller, thinner, younger replica of Lord Worster, the elder son and heir of Worster Hall at some future date, stood beaming down on his sister. "I couldn't let my two favorite girls go to London unescorted, now could I? With Papa laid up with the gout and Aunt Minnie insisting on coming for you in her own coach, I felt I was needed." His doe-brown eyes twinkled as he doffed his beaver hat in a sweeping bow to her, the early spring breeze ruffling sand-colored hair that matched a small mustache and trim Van Dyke of the same color. "My dear Carolyn, how charming you look. I predict you will take London by storm. I further wager by the end of the Season you'll have nothing less than a premier duke making Papa an offer."

"Ah, Edward, Viscount of Lynsford, flatterer *extraordinaire,* and brother *par excellence,* I thank you," Carol acknowledged with a deep curtsy, "but I fear city living has turned you into a needle-witted noddicock if you think the likes of me would have any duke, let alone a premier one, drop his handkerchief for me. 'Dooks' don't fall for country girls." The teasing glint in her merry eyes matched his and they both laughed. Then Carol turned to kiss the cheek of her aunt, telling her how glad she was to welcome her to Worster Hall.

That evening at dinner was the first time Carol heard any mention of the Duke of Overton. The viscount entertained the entire family with spicy *on dits* of the *ton.* He said all London was a-twitter because Overton had returned to England after a two-year stay in Italy. Edward was anxious to meet him as the duke was considered a whipster of the first water and a superb Corinthian. He was a member of the Four-Horse Club with a racing curricle built to his own design, and according to one of his friends who knew the duke, a prince of a fellow.

Carol noticed the guarded look that Aunt Minnie and her father exchanged, but forgot it when Lily asked if Imp was going to London, too.

At the mention of her little Yorkshire terrier,

14

Carol looked pleadingly at her aunt. "Could I take him, Aunt Minnie? He's quite small, you know, and very well-mannered. He'd be no bother, I assure you. He's not really as mischievous as his name implies."

Lady Minerva cocked her beautifully coiffed head to one side. "I hate to say nay, Carol my pet, but have you forgotten we went through all this nonsense last year. It's not that I dislike your little dog, it's just that dogs of any kind send me into sneezing fits whenever I am in close contact with them."

Carol looked down at her plate. "I'm sorry, Aunt Minnie. I did forget. Of course, I won't bring him." She turned to her younger sister and began giving instructions on how Lily should care for her darling pet. She never gave the duke another thought.

The next morning preparations began early for the trip into town, and within an hour the whole entourage was underway. Aunt Minnie, Lord Lynsford, and Lady Carolyn in the chaise and four. Flossie, Aunt Minnie's maid Martha, and all the baggage following behind in the light carriage.

Carol tried to be as lighthearted as her aunt and brother, but besides not really wanting to go, she was a bit nettled at Aunt Minnie for insisting she wear her old brown bombazine dress, and worse yet, enclose her hair in an old-fashioned lace mobcap. All her protestations were to no avail. She was told in no uncertain terms by Lady Minerva that the old dress would suffice since they did not intend to stop until they came to her London house and it would save her better traveling dress from becoming dusty. That was the reason for the mobcap, too.

It would keep her hair free of road dust. It didn't move Aunt Minnie when Carol complained that the bombazine was a shade too warm, and in the mob-cap she looked like a serving girl. Her reply to that was that the dress would guard against any chill should the wind freshen a bit, and no one would see her in the cap except family. So with a sigh, she settled back against the coach squabs. One bright spot occurred that turned the corners of her pretty mouth up into a smile. Tim, one of Aunt Minnie's postboys, nearly popped his eyes when he caught sight of young Flossie with her cornsilk-colored curls, her bright blue eyes, and cherry-red lips.

At least, Carol thought to herself as the coach-man flipped the reins for the horses to start, the trip to London may not be wasted, after all. If *I* don't find a suitable husband, young *Flossie* well might.

Chapter Two

Not only did Lady Minerva dislike driving in any other than her own vehicle, but she heartily disliked the idea of staying overnight in even the finest of public inns. She was persuaded that the previous occupants of all rooms were carriers of bugs, and she was unwilling to provide her regal person for their new abode. Though preferring to dine in her own home on food prepared by her own capable chef, she did make the concession to stop for nuncheon at The Blue Goose Inn, the half-way mark on the way to London. So it was a great relief to Lady Carolyn, whose back and arms were damp with perspiration from the heavy bombazine dress, to hear the postillions blow their yard of tin to announce their arrival at the inn.

Besides the too-warm dress, the sun had come from behind the morning clouds and was shining down unmercifully, adding to her discomfort. As Carol followed her aunt and brother into the inn, she felt as if she were wrapped in a woolen blanket instead of just being covered with sunshine. Edward made reservations for their meal while the two ladies, accompanied by Flossie and Martha, were led into the inn's parlor. Instead of finding the privacy they sought, they were pleasantly surprised to find the dowager Lady Katherine Ravenhill, a relative of theirs, sitting on the settle.

With squeals of delight, Lady Minerva and Lady Katherine embraced, both asking at the same time what the other was doing here.

"You first, Cousin Kate," Lady Minerva smiled. "Then I'll explain our presence here."

Katherine Pettigrew, widow of Aubrey Pettigrew, third Earl of Ravenhill and mother to young Troy, the fourth Earl, explained that she was accompanying her son back to London to act as his hostess for the Season. Lord Ravenhill was even now making arrangements for a room to accommodate each of them overnight. They had had the misfortune of having a tire break loose on one of their wheels, and by the time repairs could be made, it would cause them to journey to London long after dark. Her son didn't want to expose them to possible onslaughts by highwaymen. Her maid, Clara, was seeing to nuncheon.

Lady Minerva told how they were on the way to her London house, having just spent the night at her brother's home, and how she was bringing Lady Carolyn back for the Season. Just as she finished Lord Lynsford came into the room, followed by a young man about his height and build, only with dark hair and deep blue eyes.

"Look what I found! Cousin Troy, of all people, here at The Blue Goose!" By then, he'd seen Lady Ravenhill. Coming over to where she sat on the settle, he bent low and kissed her hand. "What a pleasant surprise to see you, too, Cousin Kate. You're looking in fine fettle, as usual."

She smiled and her eyes, the same blue as her son's, twinkled merrily. "What a flatterer you've become, Edward, but never mind, 'tis music to an old lady's ears." She looked him over from head to toe. "I believe you've grown taller since I saw you last Season, if that's possible. In any case, you're just like my Troy, a real Pink of the *Ton,* caring more about the cut of your coat and the arrangement of your neckcloth than finding a suitable wife to grace your table or furnish you with heirs to keep the bloodline strong. Or is it possible you already have a prospective bride in mind?"

Lord Lynsford looked over at Lord Ravenhill and both young men rolled their eyes upward in smiling forbearance at yet another reprimand on the same old theme they'd been getting from their elders in both families. "No, Cousin Kate, alas, I've no prospects in mind. It seems all the young ladies I favor don't favor me. Poor me, I really deserve your pity rather than your censure."

"Oh, stuff!" the elegant lady said, quite inelegantly.

As they all laughed, Lady Minerva's coachman came to the door. "My lady, may I have a word with you, please?"

Lady Minerva beckoned him into the room, asked if there was anything wrong. On being told he'd just discovered one of the wheelers had cast a shoe and that it would be quite some time before he could be shod, she called for Martha to bring her the vinaigrette. She knew the delay would force them to travel the major part of the way to London after dark, and like Lady Katherine, she had no desire to fall prey to highwaymen. That meant an overnight stay at the inn. She revived, however, when it was pointed out by Carol and the young men that, since both she and Cousin Kate were being inconvenienced, it was nice they had each other for company.

After nuncheon, the young men left the parlor to the ladies. Flossie and Martha and Clara were dispatched upstairs to make sure their rooms would be spotlessly clean and that no traces of former occupants remained. The two older women exchanged family news, then the conversation turned to the *on dits* of London. Carol, uncomfortably warm and feeling drowsy from too much and too rich food urged on her by her aunt and cousin, was trying to think of some reason to escape their company. She knew very few of the people they discussed and cared less. After almost an hour of raging boredom, she pleaded a headache, saying she intended going to her room and lying down with a lavender-soaked cloth to her brow.

Once out of the warm room, she decided to take a walk in the yard surrounding the inn. She had gone out the front entrance and turned the corner towards the back when she heard the sounds of a carriage of some sort being halted. She didn't bother to look around, just kept on walking, looking out towards the meadow that lay adjacent to the inn. She could see in the distance what appeared to be a small footbridge. As she drew nearer, she saw it was a bridge spanning a delightful little stream. She headed directly for it. The banks of the rippling stream were well shaded by towering oaks, and at the water's edge tender willow leaves trailed down. She crossed over the bridge, looked around at her surroundings. No one was near. That was all the excuse she needed. With eager fingers, she unbuttoned the high neck of her uncomfortable dress, opening the sides out to let the air cool her long slender neck. Next, she unbuttoned the tight narrow sleeves and rolled them up her arms as far as they would go, sighing with relief at the cooling effect. Then she did something she hadn't done since leaving the schoolroom. She sat down on the soft grass, removed her shoes and stocking and dipped her feet in the cool rippling waters of the stream. Ah, what bliss, she thought, after being so terribly warm in that odious old dress. With a rebellious gesture, she snatched off the lace mobcap, letting her thick chestnut hair tumble down her back. If Aunt Minnie could see her now, she'd faint for sure, but at the moment

Carol didn't care. When she was sufficiently cooled off, she would straighten herself up and go back to the inn in proper manner. Meantime, she relaxed. As she thought back to all the gossip her aunt and cousin had exchanged, she grew a bit more belligerent about having to go through another Season. Against all the really pretty girls to be presented to Society, what chance did she have to find a husband suitable enough for her father? She felt in her bones it would just be a repeat of last year—either she'd attract OLD men or FORTUNE-HUNTERS. Besides, she didn't care a whit about all the goings-on that Aunt Minnie and Cousin Kate considered such juicy morsels. So Lady Winthrop gave Lady Montague the cut direct? Who cared? Neither was she interested in Prinny, that fat middle-aged royal rogue, and his crowd of fawning sycophants. She had to admit her interest was piqued a bit when the ladies talked about James Farrell, Duke of Overton, and his late wife's sordid love affair. No doubt that was the reason for the guarded look that passed between Aunt Minnie and Lord Worster at supper last evening when Edward had mentioned the duke was back in England.

It was strange to think that a young woman of good family with seemingly everything to make her happy—a handsome wealthy husband with a title and a beautiful baby son—would leave it all to run away with a young rake-shame who was definitely not *bon ton*. She was equally fascinated with the rest of the tale. The young ne'er-do-well was a contemporary of the duke, but unlike James Farrell had been in one unsavory escapade after another since the age of fourteen. His father, a friend of the

21

elder Overton, had persuaded James to let his son be a guest at the Castle until his latest scandalous episode died down and gossipy tongues ceased to wag. Apparently, he had charmed his way into the heart of the duke's young wife so much so that she decided to give up everything she had to follow him. If an old and trusted servant who had served the duke's family long and well had not overheard their plans and sent for the duke, the two lovers might have gotten away. Instead, a tragedy occurred.

According to the servant, the young duchess and her paramour set out for a leisurely horseback ride in the countryside, but it was just a smoke screen to cover their real intentions. The young rake-shame had a coach and four waiting at a nearby tavern with the lady's packed portmanteau already inside. As soon as they were out of sight of the Castle, they planned to race to the waiting coach, leave their horses at the tavern, and speed away to Ramsgate where they planned to cross the Channel and from a French port book passage to America. The minute the pair rode out of the courtyard, the servant sent a groom on a fast horse to fetch the duke, who was at the farthest end of his estate overseeing the erection of a new hunting lodge. After receiving the groom's message, he whirled his horse around and sped off in pursuit of his fleeing wife. He was able to overtake them before they reached the waiting coach. As the duke came into view behind them, the wife's lover fired his pistol at him, but the duke kept enough distance between them for his shots to miss the mark. When he knew the fleeing man's pistol was empty, he sprang his mount, catching up to them and commanding them to halt with his own pistol leveled at them. Then the duke, being an honorable man and knowing his erstwhile friend's pistol was without bullets, requested him to draw his sword, demanding satisfaction in a duel. His wife, still mounted on her horse, witnessed the duel in which the duke was the victor. Seeing her lover dead, she whirled her horse around so sharply that the horse was thrown off balance and stumbled, causing the lady to lose her seat. She fell to the ground in some freak manner that broke her neck, and she, too, died instantly. This all took place seven years ago, and for most of that time the duke has been out of England traveling the globe. Now he is back in residence at Overton Castle, and the word is out that he is coming to his London house for the Season to launch his only sister who has just now turned eighteen. The word is also out that he hopes to escape designing mamas and their marriageable daughters because he has no plans to ever marry again. He has his heir, and no end of any kind of female companionship he might desire.

Humph! Carol thought to herself as she wiggled her feet in the cool gurgling water, he must be a very egotistical person to think EVERY female he meets wants him for a husband. Without even knowing him, she was sure SHE would not fall prey to his charms, providing he had any.

The relief from the heat, the soft sounds of the babbling brook and the delicate odor of small wildflowers relaxed and soothed her disquieted spirit. She felt at peace with the world again. She leaned back against the trunk of one of the oak trees and without intending to do so, fell asleep, her feet still dangling in the shallow stream.

Chapter Three

At the same moment Lady Carolyn rounded the corner of The Blue Goose Inn, a crested paneled curricle drawn by a spirited pair of blood-chestnuts halted at the front. The driver, James Ogden Farrell, fifth Duke of Overton, alighted, carelessly threw the reins to his tiger along with his many-caped driving coat, and walked inside. With much bowing and scraping by the innkeeper, he was seated at a table near a window and a tankard of ale set before him. His black brows knitted slightly and his ebony eyes held a worried look. After a sip or two of the ale, he looked out the window, not really seeing the view outside, but seeing instead, in his mind, the pinched little face of his seven-year-old son, Robert.

For the first few years after Margaret died, he could hardly bear to be around their son whose blue liquid eyes and curly blond hair was a stabbing reminder of her and her infamous infidelity. But these last two years, whenever he'd made a stop-over at the Castle on his way to some other part of the globe, he'd begun to see something of himself in the child and he began to feel a bit closer to him. But damme! Every time he tried to come near the child, he'd hide behind the skirts of his nanny, or the dowager duchess, or Laura. The boy acted as if he were desperately afraid of him. He'd tried to talk to his mother, the duchess, about Robert, but he always heard the same advice—get the child a mother, that's what he needs. And he always gave back the same answer. Though he was completely over his love for Margaret and the hurt of her betrayal, he never intended to marry again. He would never place himself in such a vulnerable position again. But, he thought taking another sip of his ale, he would have to do SOMETHING. He couldn't let his only son and heir stand in fear of him.

Then the thought of Laura caused another furrow in his brow. He knew it was his place as the only remaining adult male in the family to see his young sister through her first London Season, but it really rubbed against the grain. He had no desire to go through all the motions of seeming to enjoy himself as he escorted Laura to and from all the invitations she'd get as the sister of the Duke of Overton. But, remembering his father's dying words, he knew he'd do it. As the elder Overton lay dying, he'd made James promise to look after his mother and sister.

"If your older brother hadn't been thrown by his horse, and your younger brother hadn't succumbed to the fever, you wouldn't have had all the responsibility, James, but it happened, and when I'm gone, you'll inherit my title and lands and all the duties they entail. I'm counting on you to do your very best." His father had then closed his eyes for a moment or two. Suddenly, he opened them, clasped his son's hand and said, "Take care of your mother, son, and my darling little daughter." With that, he lay back on his pillow and expired.

Well, that little daughter was now eighteen with hair like strained honey, eyes like dazzling sapphires, and the sweetest disposition in all England. It wasn't simply introducing Laura to Society that galled him. It was the fact that his presence in London would set tongues to wagging again about his unhappy marriage and the scandalous way it ended. More than that, without being toplofty, but just facing facts, he knew that he himself would be the target of designing mamas and ambitious daughters even more than Laura would of admiring suitors. That's what really annoyed him. Well, he thought emptying the last of the ale from the tankard, I'll go through with it, but no law says I have to like it.

Refusing the offer of a second tankard, he rose and went back outside. Liam, his trusted tiger, was standing guard beside the curricle, his thick shock of red hair and generous sprinkling of freckles shining in the bright sunlight. His wide mouth split into a lazy grin at sight of the duke. "Ready to go, sir?"

"Not just yet, Liam. I think I'll walk about, stretch my legs a bit," the duke said, undoing his fashionably wrapped neckcloth and removing his frock-coat. As he threw the items of clothing to Liam, he mopped his face with a handkerchief. "I say, it's devilishly hot for this time of year. Feels more like summer than early spring." He turned, calling back over his broad shoulders, "You'll have time for another pint if you'd like before I return."

With that, he took the same path as did Lady Carolyn, seeing in the distance the same little footbridge and setting his booted feet in that direction.

Lady Carolyn's brief snooze ended abruptly bringing her back to consciousness, though her eyes remained closed. She had that eerie feeling that she was being observed, and a cold chill snaked down her back. With trepidation she lifted her lids, her topaz eyes widening at the sight of the tall lean-waisted, broad-shouldered stranger who leaned languidly against the railing of the little bridge, his dark eyes fastened on her intently.

She drew in her breath at the sight of him. His black hair trimmed in a Brutus cut above an angular sardonic face tanned bronze by a searing sun frightened her; at the same time she experienced a strange new feeling, something akin to admiration. He reminded her of fabled kings who plundered recklessly and brooked no opposition. Becoming conscious of her state of dishabille, she hurriedly jerked her bare feet from the stream, scrambled to stand upright, smoothing her dress down, trying to cover as much of her exposed limbs as possible.

A sudden humorous glint flickered in the man's penetrating eyes. "Ah, Sleeping Beauty," he said, mockingly, "you've cheated me. I was about to play Prince Charming and awaken you with a kiss."

"Sir!" Carol cried. "How dare you speak to me in that degrading manner! I'm not who you may think I am."

Supposing her to be a bar-maid from the inn, he decided to go along with the game. "Oh?" he said, one heavy brow quirked upward. "And just who may you be? Not the Queen in disguise, for you are surely younger and much prettier than she is. And no lady, either, methinks." His ebony eyes raked over her, taking in the unbuttoned neckline, the rolled-up sleeves, the loose flowing hair that tumbled about her shoulders, and the lace mob-cap—that well-known badge of maids and serving girls. He slowly straightened to his full towering height, stepped from the bridge to within inches from her.

"And would a kiss be so terrible, my pretty one? Surely, it would cost you nothing and enrich me bountifully." He smiled down at her, and it was like the sun emerging from a cloud. No more did his face hold that arrogant sinister look. Instead, his smile kindled his cold eyes with warmth, gave to his countenance a radiant glow.

But to Carol it brought only anger. He thought she was some *lightskirt* to be taken in by flattery and cajolery. Well, she'd soon put a stop to *that* nonsense! Drawing herself up to *her* full height, she said, "Whatever you may think of me, 'tis certain *you're* no *gentleman*." Her anger-blazed eyes looked at his snowy white shirt opened enough to show a glimpse of curly black chest hair. His buck-skins and top boots were slightly salted with dust, the typical attire of a country-bred man. "Not even a country bumpkin would be so discourteous to a female whether she be serving girl or a lady of rank. But," she said, trying to move past him, "I doubt that you've had much experience with the latter."

He caught her wrist, staying her in her tracks. "Oh, come now, Golden Eyes, don't put on such airs with me. You'll never catch a husband that way. Men like girls whose words are coated with honey, not acid."

For some reason she was never to explain to herself, she blurted, "I've no intention of catching a husband. I intend to remain in the single state for the rest of my life."

"Oh, that'd never do! Think of what you'd miss." Before she could bat an eye, he had pulled her to him, his strong arms holding her fast. "Here's just a sample of what you'd miss," he said, lowering his head and capturing her lips with his. It was not an asking kiss; it demanded, and expertly.

Carol's head began to swim, she tried to struggle against him, but was held too fast. She felt his heart throb against hers, even through her bombazine dress. Then a new and alien feeling washed over her and for a moment she trembled against him, and he sensed it. His embrace relaxed and as he lifted his mouth from hers, a low chuckle rumbled from his throat.

It was that knowing laugh that rubbed her raw. For one wild moment she had returned his kiss and he was fully aware of it! She wanted to die with the shame of it. Pushing against him with all her might, she fully intended to slap his wicked face, but she didn't get the chance. From the force of her shove, her bare feet slipped on the muddy bank and before she could gain her balance, she fell backwards into the stream, sitting down rather hard in its shallow depth.

The dark-eyed stranger threw back his head and laughed, a booming sound that rent asunder the serenity of the tree-shaded bower. Holding out a hand, he said, "I've heard of kisses that knocked a lady off her feet, but it never happened to me before. Here, let me help you up and see if I can have the same results again."

"Oh! You odious beast! I'd rather stay right here than be subjected to THAT again! And you can believe me when I tell you it was not your kiss that brought me low, but that muddy bank. If I'd been able to keep my footing, you'd have felt the sting of my palm against your smirking face."

"In that case, Mistress," he said, his eyes now void of laughter, "I shall leave you to your watery seat. I hope you enjoy it."

Never had Carol been so angry as she watched his departing figure. Not only angry at his arrogant treatment of her, but at herself for not handling the situation better than she did. Gentleman or country bumpkin, she had the feeling he meant her no harm, was only teasing her. If she'd responded like she would have had it been Edward or Troy, it wouldn't have ended this way. They would have had a bit of light conversation and then gone their separate ways. As she scrambled up the bank and tried to wring as much water as possible out of her dress, she seemed to hear again his deep voice calling her "my pretty one." And without volition, her heart skipped a beat. But as fleetingly as the thought came, it left. No doubt, he called all females that. The more she thought on it, the angrier she became. Even serving girls deserved better treatment than that! And to be fair, which Carol prided herself to be, if he took her for an easy conquest, it was as much her fault as his, seeing as how she looked—dress pulled up to her knees, bare feet

30

dangling in the water, hair loose and flowing down her back. If she'd gone to her room as she told Aunt Minnie she was going, she wouldn't be in this embarrassing position. Now, if she could only slip into the back of the inn and up to her room without seeing anyone, she would keep secret her encounter with the boorish stranger.

The cook let her in the kitchen, accepted the excuse that she fell into the stream, and showed her the back stairs so she made it to her room without notice. But it wasn't that easy to fend off Flossie's probing questions and searching glances. Finally, after the third time Flossie had said, "Lud, Ma'am, cooling your feet in the water, I can understand, but how you could fall backwards into the stream still holding your lace cap in one hand and your shoes and stockings in the other, is a mystery to me. Wasn't there anyone around to help you?" Carol decided to tell her the truth.

"If you must know, yes, there *was* someone, but I refused his help after the cavalier way he treated me. In fact, he was the cause of my falling. I was trying to push myself away from his embrace when I lost my footing in the mud."

"His embrace! Lud, Ma'am, what did he do to you? Why didn't you scream for help?" Flossie's eyes were like round blue saucers as she wondered what stranger had the boldness to even speak to her ladyship, let alone touch her noble person. "Who was this man? Had you ever seen him before?"

"No, and I hope I never shall again. He—he—he kissed me!" Carol said, a warm flush spreading over her face as she remembered the feel of his lips on hers. Was it shame she felt or something else?

31

She wondered. And, come to think of it, why *didn't* she scream for help?

Flossie's reply interrupted these errant thoughts by saying, "Lud! Do you think he's still around? Don't you think you ought to send Coachman to see if he can find him and bring him to taw?"

"No! I don't want anybody to know of this! He's either some country squire with licentious morals or a brazen highwayman. Either one, I'm sure he's far away by now. And I don't want to hear anymore about it." She began removing the sodden dress and petticoats. "See if you can arrange a bath for me and have my supper sent up on a tray. I don't intend to venture from this room until we leave in the morning."

After Flossie had spread out her lady's wet clothes to dry, she went down to see about hot water and food. Carol looked out the window towards the back. She could see the footbridge in the distance. Once again she thought of the stranger's kiss.

Only once before had she been kissed by a man other than her father or brothers. Last Season she had allowed that fortune-hunting Mr. Carraway to kiss her, but it was nothing like the one the stranger gave her. And she didn't react to Mr. Carraway's kiss the way she did to the stranger's, either. Why? What made the difference? With these thoughts whirling around in her mind, she went over to the bed and lay down. This time she really did have a headache.

Lord Ravenhill and his mother were the first to go the next morning. Their carriage pulled out, the tire having been repaired while they slept, amid exchanged farewells and promises to visit as soon as both families were settled into their respective London houses. Then, the horse properly shod, Lady Minerva's two carriages were loaded. Aunt Minnie and Carol with their abigails sat in the inn's parlor until time to leave. Lord Lynsford joined them, his eyes bright as a newly-minted guinea. "I say, Carol, you picked a most inopportune time to have a headache. Had you stayed with Aunt Minnie and Cousin Kate, you'd have been presented to the Duke of Overton. Imagine! Not only did we have the good fortune to meet up with Troy and Cousin Kate here at the inn, but His Grace the Duke, too. He's going to see that his London house is properly staffed and ready for his mother and sister who will stay through the Season. They will arrive next week in time for the first Assembly at Almack's. I'm really looking forward to meeting the sister."

"Yes, and it was also fortunate that Troy was already acquainted with the duke and was able to introduce us. Otherwise, we may have never met," added Aunt Minnie. "He was a most charming man. He'll make a fine catch for some suitable lady. It was certainly not his fault his late wife brought such disgrace to the family's proud name." She looked over to her niece. "However, Carol dear, I wouldn't want you to set *your* cap for him. He's far too old for you. Not a day under thirty-four is my guess."

As Edward and her aunt talked, Carol had a sinking feeling in the pit of her stomach. The Duke of Overton! Could he have been the stranger on the bridge? Now that the shameful episode was behind her, she could look on it with more discernment. At the time, she only looked at the man himself, but now, listening to her brother and aunt extol his virtues, she remembered the expert tailoring of his buckskins, the fine cambric of his snowy white shirt, and the expensive cut of his boots. For sure, he was no ordinary country squire as she had thought. Nor was he a rough highwayman, either. But the Duke of Overton? Good God! She sincerely hoped not, for that would mean she'd be forced to meet him again at some social function. No! she told herself, it just couldn't have been him, but when she happened to glance toward Flossie, she could see her own thoughts mirrored in Flossie's eyes, too.

"W-w-what did the duke look like? I mean— uh—does he show his advanced age much?" Carol managed to ask, hoping against hope that she'd be told he looked quite old, not at all with the young handsome face that had stared down at her.

"Advanced age! Don't be such a pea-goose, Carol. Thirty-four may be a bit old for a nineteen-year-old girl like you, but he's a far cry from being a doddering old man. He's a true Corinthian and quite attractive. Wouldn't you say so, Aunt Minnie?" responded Edward.

"Yes," Lady Minerva answered, "I suppose he could be considered handsome in a very masculine way, though such a tall, dark-visaged man with a hawk-like nose and such penetrating black eyes doesn't appeal to me as much as a lighter-colored man. Still, I'm sure there are those who would fall victim to his charms, not to mention three estates and an income of forty thousand pounds a year. *And* a title!"

Edward laughed. "Ah, always the practical one, aren't you, Aunt Minnie?"

Before an answer could be given, Coachman came to assist them to the carriage. With a sinking feeling Carol mounted the steps. The description was too accurate—tall, black eyes, dark-visaged, hawk-like nose—to be that of any other. It had to be the duke who had kissed her! And she would have to meet him as if she'd never seen him before. Oh! What an ODIOUS man! He might be the *premier parti* of the *ton*, but not to her. To her, he was an enemy!

Chapter Four

As soon as they arrived at the Simms's house in Berkeley Square, Aunt Minnie assembled all the staff. There was Avery, the butler, standing just as tall and straight and solemn as he did last year. Carol wondered if even his undergarments were as stiffly starched as his shirts and collars. Next, came Mrs. Willard, generalissimo of the domestic staff. Her gray dress matched her gray hair and her face was almost as porcelain-white as her organdy apron and matching collar and cuffs. Carol had seen her smile twice last Season and looked forward to seeing if there'd be a repeat performance this year. The house maids were standing neatly in a row, behind them was Cook with her staff of kitchen help. Cook was a large-boned woman whose broad face bore dry paths of past laughter, a woman who had a lust for life and to whom the creating of good food was a special calling. But even she was solemn on this occasion. Lady Minerva introduced Carol to the two new maids who had been hired since last Season and renewed Carol's acquaintance with all the rest of the staff. Flossie was introduced and assigned her room. After the exchange of a few pleasant amenities, all were dismissed and Lady Minerva and Lady Carolyn went to their rooms to freshen up.

Carol was quite impressed with her aunt. She made sure the key positions were filled by competent people and looked to them to see that everything functioned smoothly and properly. Only on very rare occasions was it necessary for Lady Minerva to interfere with domestic management.

Flossie was equally impressed, though for a different reason. For the first time in her short life, she'd be able to take things easy. It was no trouble for her to arrange Lady Carolyn's hair and see that all her clothes were kept in proper order, especially after all the chores she'd had to do at home. Now, with a room to herself, her meals prepared for her by somebody else and with no washing and mopping to do, she was in seventh heaven. There was just one thing that worried her—her father's illness back home. She was still thinking about him when she went to assist her ladyship to dress for dinner.

Facing the mirror as Flossie arranged her hair, Carol saw the blue eyes clouded with worry and the usually laughing cherry-red mouth pressed into a grim line. "What's the matter, Flossie? Are you displeased with arrangements here at Aunt Minnie's?" Carol asked.

"Oh, no! Ma'am, I'm pleased as Punch, it's just that—that—well, I'm worried about Pa. I wish I could get word of him now and then. Also, I wish I could let him and Mum know that I'm doing all right, too." She gave a sigh. " 'Twill be a long time before we go back to Worster, you know."

"Why, Flossie, you won't have to stay out of touch with your father and mother until we return. I intend to write my father a letter every week and send it by one of the grooms. You can do the same, and a Worster Hall groom can bring us replies. That way you can . . ." Carol's voice faded away at the distressed look that shadowed Flossie's pert face. Oh, dear, thought Carol, I've really put my foot in my mouth this time. The poor little thing probably can't read nor write, neither can her mother and father, and she's too embarrassed to say so. "Or better yet," Carol went on to say, pretending she'd just had a much better inspiration, "when I write my letters, you can tell me anything you want to say and I'll write it down for you, and Papa can tell George and Ada all the news at one time. Then when he replies, he can tell us all the news about Worster Hall and the progress your father is making towards regaining his health. How does that sound to you?"

"Oh, Ma'am!" Flossie replied, her lips curving in a smile and the sparkle back in her eyes. "I'd be ever so grateful to you 'cause what with my duties and all, I might be hard pressed to find enough time to write myself." Flossie's heart swelled to near bursting to think her ladyship considered her worthy of such a special favor. Not only that, but Lady Carolyn no doubt suspected she and Mum and Pa couldn't do much more than read and write their own names, but was too kind to bring it up. At that moment if Carol had realized the devotion that emitted from the heart of that sixteen-year-old girl at her little act of kindness, she would have been quite humbled.

As Flossie completed dressing her hair *à la diadème,* Carol turned to her, smiling. "And speaking of grooms, I think I know a particular grooms-man who would jump at the chance to run an errand for you."

Flossie's face turned pink. She lowered her eyes, black lashes fanning her soft cheeks. "Whatever do you mean, Ma'am? I'm sure I don't know who you have in mind."

Carol laughed. "I'm sure you do, Flossie. You were quite aware of young Tim's eyes on you as we left the Hall *and* the inn."

Flossie lifted her shining eyes, smiled a bit saucily. "Well, yes, I did notice a little, but I just thought that was because mine was a new face, one he hadn't seen before."

"Stuff!" laughed Carol. "He was admiring you and you know it. You watch your step, though, Flossie. I don't want Ada blaming me for a romance of which she might not approve."

"Don't you worry, Ma'am. I don't intend to give my heart and hand to the first man I meet. Besides, Tim's just a boy. When I get ready to settle down with a husband, I want one that's full grown."

Carol thought Flossie showed uncommon good sense and she felt a bit easier about bringing her to London, but before she could tell her so, the ormolu clock on the mantel chimed the dinner hour and she hurriedly left to join her aunt in the dining room.

The next several days were busy ones indeed. The ladies made several trips to Bond Street to pore over the latest fashion plates and fabrics at various establishments. They purchased slippers and gloves, silk stocking, ribbons and feathers for their hair and a few new bonnets. Once or twice Lady Katherine joined them on their shopping trips, but Carol noticed Cousin Kate made very few purchases. She wondered why. Surely, Lord Ravenhill, with the income he had, could well afford to buy his mother anything she wanted. But in the excitement of her own new things, she dismissed Cousin Kate's paucity of purchases as just due to the fact that she no longer took much pleasure in new things.

Underlying all the activity and the few small informal evening parties to which they'd been invited, there was a small nagging thought that plagued Carol's mind. How would she face the duke at the opening assembly at Almack's? She knew he'd be there to present his sister to the Patronesses. Would he recognize her as the sleeping disheveled girl by the stream, and if so, what should she say to him? What would he say to her? As the day grew nearer, her anxiety loomed greater and greater until it overshadowed what pleasure she might have taken in the opening ball of the Season.

However, when the day finally arrived and Edward came to escort her and Lady Minerva to Almack's, she almost forgot her dread at the gleam in her brother's eyes as she came down the curving stairs to greet him.

"My dear sister," said Edward, making a sweeping bow, "you dazzle these old eyes of mine. Last year you were just another girl among all the others, but now! I vow, I'll be hard pressed to protect you from all the swains that'll clamor for your attention."

Without vanity, but with feminine intuition, she knew she'd never looked better. The reflection she'd just left in the mirror confirmed that. Her new emerald green figured brocade dress complimented her slightly sun-kissed face and the stylish *Méduse* hair arrangement showed her shiny chestnut tresses to great advantage. On a closer look at her face in the mirror, she saw the candlegleam highlighted her gold-dappled eyes. Tonight she bore no resemblance to that untidy girl in the old bombazine dress. There was a chance the duke wouldn't connect the two as the same person. So, with a lighter heart and taking her cue from her brother's teasing banter, she replied, "Thank you, Brother dear, and you look like an Exquisite! Those black satin breeches and swallowtail coat of gray superfine make you look like a macaroni. Have you learned to mince yet?"

He raised his quizzing glass lanquidly and gazed archly at her. "Keep a civil tongue in your head or I may turn around and leave you and Aunt Minnie without an escort."

They laughed together as was their wont since

childhood. Besides being brother and sister they were good friends, and each knew the other could be depended on whenever a demanding occasion arose. Carol laid a soft hand on his sleeve.

"You wouldn't do that to me, would you, Edward?" Her eyes sparkled and her mouth curved sweetly in a winsome smile.

Edward looked down at her. "I guess not, Golden Eyes, but you can't call me names and get away with it."

Carol was glad she didn't have to answer, for at his teasing appellation all her anxiety returned, chasing away all other thoughts. The duke had called her Golden Eyes! Would they be the means by which he'd recognize her?

Just then Lady Minerva joined them and Edward escorted both out to his waiting carriage. When they pulled into King Street and stopped at Almack's, Carol was hoping she'd faint and have to be carried back to the Berkeley Square house.

She revived considerably when, on looking searchingly around the room, she didn't see any sign of the duke's dark-visaged face. And as the Patronesses beamed their welcome on her and began presenting various Pinks of the *ton* who were eager to write their names on her dance card, she began to smile and unbend a bit.

Besides her fear of meeting the Duke of Overton, she'd harbored another misgiving—the disapproval of the Patronesses in coming for her second Season. But they couldn't have been nicer, inquiring after her father's health and that of young Oliver and Lily who were still back at Worster Hall, and generally making her feel quite at ease. She wasn't sure

41

whether it was for herself alone or because she was a daughter of a wealthy marquis or because she had an eligible brother who would someday inherit that same title and wealth. In any case, she decided, she'd take advantage of it and simply enjoy it as her father urged her to do.

She had just finished dancing the *Boulengère* with a mild-mannered, sandy-haired young man and he was escorting her back to Aunt Minnie when she stopped dead in her tracks. Her dancing partner looked startled, asked, "Is something amiss, Lady Carolyn? You're not ill, are you?"

Recovering from her surprise at the people grouped around Lady Minerva and Viscount Lynsford, she tried to recapture her *sang-froid*. "Why—ah—no, I'm not ill. I—I—stumbled a bit. I—ah—I think perhaps there might have been a pebble on the floor, though I can't imagine how such a thing came to be." She forced a smile. "But I have my balance now, thank you." With that, she resumed her steps towards her family, wishing she'd faint, die, disappear, anything to keep from being presented to that darkly handsome face whose mouth was curled in a cynical smile and whose ebony eyes held a mocking glint. Oh yes, she had recognized him instantly. He stood two or three inches above Edward's tall frame and that of Lord Ravenhill's and seemed to tower over the four ladies—Aunt Minnie, Cousin Kate, a beautiful young girl whose hair gleamed in the light like a gold sovereign, and another lady about the age of Carol's aunt. No doubt his mother and sister. Edward or someone in the family must have pointed her out, because the duke's amused eyes followed her until she and her escort reached the little group.

The sandy-haired young man handed her back to her aunt, then hastily took his leave. Edward took hold of her hand, led her over to the elegantly gowned lady. As Carol suspected, she was the Dowager Duchess, and the girl to whom she was presented next was Lady Laura, the Duke's young sister. Carol was sure Lady Laura would have a successful Season. She had all the approved attributes of the *ton*—blonde curls, eyes like clear sapphires, a shy maidenly manner, and a sweet smile.

Next, Edward presented her to His Grace the Duke. She was forced by custom to look up into those dark mocking eyes. He took her outstretched hand in his, bowed as he brought her cold fingers to his warm lips and planted a light kiss on the back of her hand, all the time his eyes looking steadily into hers.

"I'm charmed to finally make your acquaintance, Lady Carolyn. I understand you were at The Blue Goose Inn where I met your distinguished family, but that you were indisposed by a headache. I trust you are quite well now and suffer no results from your short stay at the inn."

Oh! What an odious man, she thought, feeling a warm flush spread over her neck and face. He *knew* she was the girl who had returned his kiss and was laughing at her!

Summing up as much *hauteur* as she could manage, she said, icily, "I'm very well, thank you." She said nothing else, no polite words, no expression of pleasure in meeting him. She withdrew her hand from his, turned to Lady Katherine and began to inquire if she was comfortably settled in at Lord

Ravenhill's house. She noted the surprised look in Aunt Minnie's eyes at her cool treatment of the duke, but pretended she didn't. Somehow, as the group seated themselves, she found herself sitting next to Lady Laura. At the lady's other side both Edward and Troy vied for her attention and tried to claim as many dances as possible.

"The next set will be a waltz," Lord Ravenhill said, smiling at the blue-eyed girl. "Will you give me the pleasure of dancing it with you?"

Before the girl could answer, and in rather stiff and formal tones, the duke said, "Lady Laura hasn't been approved for the waltz yet. She may dance only those dances for which she's been approved."

He looked coolly into Lord Ravenhill's eyes and there was no smile on his arrogant sun-darkened face. It doesn't appear that he has any friendship for Troy, Carol thought to herself. But immediately decided she must be wrong. He was merely taking a brotherly interest in his young sister, making sure she did nothing to which the Patronesses could object. Still, at the sudden flush that spread over Troy's handsome young face, she wasn't sure she'd been mistaken. Yet what could he possibly have against her cousin since, according to Troy, they were just the barest of acquaintances? Her attention was drawn back to Lady Laura who said, demurely, "Since I'm unable to waltz with either of you two gentlemen, would both of you be kind and bring some refreshments? Then the three of us could sit together in conversation."

Carol smothered a smile behind her silk fan. The Lady Laura was all a modest young maiden should

44

be, but she was no ninnyhammer. Behind those round innocent-looking blue eyes was a young woman with the innate wisdom of knowing how to please people, especially men, yet at the same time bend them sweetly to her will. If the haughty duke thought his little sister's Season would be an easy one, he'd better think twice.

As Lord Ravenhill and Viscount Lynsford hurried off to fetch either glasses of lemonade or orgeat—the only two liquids allowed at Almack's—Overton smiled down at Carol and said,

"I trust you have been approved to waltz."

Just as he had spoken up for his sister, Aunt Minnie spoke up for her. "Oh yes, Your Grace, Lady Carolyn can waltz. She was approved last Season."

His smile widened. "Then will you do me the honor of waltzing with me?"

Oh, how she wanted to refuse! But she dared not. Aunt Minnie would wonder at her impoliteness. So would Cousin Kate. And she certainly couldn't tell them, couldn't tell anyone about that disgraceful scene that occurred on the banks of the stream behind the inn. To her further annoyance, she could tell by the laughter lurking in his sparkling jet eyes that the duke knew of the struggle going on in her mind.

Giving him her hand, she walked with him onto the dance floor. She felt all the eyes of the crowd upon them, particularly those of the Patronesses and those mothers with marriageable daughters. She conceded they did make a strikingly colorful pair. His brown velvet coat was of the Continental design and showed off his broad shoulders and narrow waist to advantage. His gold satin knee breeches molded straight muscled thighs and his well-shaped legs were encased in creamy silk stockings that matched the fall of Mechlin lace at his wrists and throat. He wore no embellishments except a large gold-encrusted emerald ring on his right index finger. Against her own green brocaded gown, his ensemble was the perfect complement. The music started and his strong arm encircled her waist.

He guided her gently but firmly in the rhythmic steps, and for a moment, as they whirled around the room, she thought back to that other time he had held her in his arms and she could almost feel the touch of his lips on hers. Drawing in her breath and giving her head a slight shake, as if to clear it of such errant thoughts, she pressed her mouth into a straight line and tried to concentrate only on the dance.

Again the duke seemed to read her mind. Smiling down at her, he said, low, "My dear Lady Carolyn, does my dancing displease you or are you disturbed by something else? Memories, perhaps? Your lovely face looks as pinched as if you'd eaten a lemon."

Her topaz eyes glared up at him. "I am not disturbed. I am angry, and you know full well why."

"I do? Whatever makes you think such a thing?" he said, a wicked twitch to his eyebrows. "We have only just met. I know nothing about you except that you are very beautiful and you dance exceptionally well."

Could he possibly be telling the truth? Was it really plausible that he didn't connect her with that bare-footed girl by the stream?

"I—I—thought we had met before under rather —ah—peculiar circumstances," she replied haltingly. Then lifting her head a bit higher so that her eyes bored into his, she said, "Am I mistaken? Have we ever met before?" She wanted to bring it out into the open, get the uncertainty over with once and for all. That way, she'd know whether to give him the cut direct or treat him with the deference his rank demanded.

But it wasn't to be that easy.

Overton smiled down at her for a full minute as they began a second turn of the room, his white even teeth in deep contrast against the sun-bronzed texture of his face. She felt her nerves twitch at his prolonged look. Then just as she felt she could stand his gaze no longer, he said, "Lady Carolyn, had I met you before under any circumstance, you can be assured I'd never forget such a lovely face as yours. I envy the man for whom you've mistaken me. He evidently has spent more time with you than I, but with your permission, I intend to make up for that loss."

Oh, what a farradiddle! She didn't know which way to turn. She didn't dare go into detail about their first meeting for fear he really was telling the truth and didn't recognize her. And she couldn't very well shun him nor any invitations he might issue without causing her aunt and brother to wonder why she was so ungracious. She had really jumped from the frying pan into the fire now.

She lowered her eyes, unaware how sweetly her dark lashes arced against her cream-colored cheeks.

"I—I—collect possibly I was mistaken. Please accept my apologies."

His arm drew her a mite closer. His deep voice whispered against her hair. "To be sure, Lady Carolyn, I'd accept anything from you, even, perish the thought, the sting of your palm on my face."

She stiffened, almost missed a step as he uttered the tender words. And the low chuckle she heard as his face brushed against her hair infuriated her. Did he recognize her or did he not? If he did, he mocked her concerning her desire to sting his face with the palm of her hand by flinging her very own words to *him* back at *her*. If he did not recognize her, then he was being overtly rude with his libertine compliments. Either way, she thought him an odious man and wished this dance to be over.

The dance did come to an end, but she didn't rid herself of his presence. As he brought her back to her aunt and brother, he continued to stand there smiling down at the whole group. He gallantly asked his mother for the next dance, but with a laugh she refused, saying too many years and too much flesh had accumulated on her bones. Then he surprised Carol by suggesting she save the supper dance for him.

She looked up at him and said, coolly, "I have already accepted my brother's kind offer for that dance and for his company at the supper table." She figured that would be the end of that! Not so. She didn't count on his persistence.

He looked over to where Edward and Troy were still engaged in vying for his sister's attention. With an amused smile, he countered, "I doubt that he'll mind exchanging places with me. He seems totally committed to the task at hand." With that, he turned directly to Edward. "Lord Lynsford, would you like permission to escort Lady Laura and the duchess in to supper?"

Edward turned a smiling face up to him. "Indeed I would, Your Grace, if it's acceptable to the ladies." He beamed a tender look at the shining blue eyes that were raised to meet his glance.

"Thank you," Lady Laura said, softly, "I shall be honored to be your supper partner. And I'm sure Mama agrees, too." She looked over at the duchess who remained silent but nodded her consent.

Troy looked daggers at the duke, but had the good sense not to voice his disappointment. And at the duke's next suggestion, he could do nothing but acquiesce politely.

"That will leave you free, Lord Ravenhill, to escort Lady Katherine and Lady Minerva, two of the most charming ladies in the whole Assembly. I'm sure you're agreeable to this distinct honor," Overton said, still smiling but whose jet eyes bore down into Troy's angry blue ones, daring him to show dissent. Thus, with smooth ruthlessness, he arranged things to suit himself, and in such a way that no one thought it anything but chivalrous.

"Now that's settled, I'll go make arrangements for a table to accommodate the eight of us," Overton said, lifting Lady Carolyn's hand to his lips. "Thank you, dear lady, for the waltz. You're an exceptionally fine dancer." As he bent his head to bestow a kiss to the back of her hand, he said, low, "I'll return very shortly, my dear."

Through gritted teeth, she answered him in the

same *sotto voce*. "You needn't hurry on my account."

"How very charming you are," he replied, a sardonic smile curling his well-shaped mouth.

It was all she could do to remain still and poised as she glared at his departing back.

Chapter Five

Sunlight flooded the room as Flossie pulled back the heavy velvet drapes. Carol's eyes, which had been staring into the shaded darkness since dawn, were suddenly squeezed shut against the brightness.

"Oh, ma'am," said Flossie, "It's sorry I am to disturb you, but I thought you were already awake. Shall I pull the drapes again and let you snooze a bit longer?"

"No, Flossie," Carol said, pulling herself up and swinging her feet to dangle at the side of her bed. "I was awake. I just shut my eyes against the sunlight. I've been awake a long time, just lying here thinking."

Putting satin slippers on her ladyship's feet and holding out a peignoir for her to slip into, Flossie smiled at her. "I don't doubt you couldn't sleep too much, ma'am, what with all the excitement over last night's ball. I'm sure you had the loveliest time ever."

"Well, you're wrong. I had a miserable time."

"Oh, I'm sorry, ma'am. Whatever happened?"

"That odious Duke of Overton ruined everything. It was as we both feared, Flossie, the duke was the man I encountered behind The Blue Goose Inn."

Flossie's mouth formed an *O* and her blue eyes opened wide. "Lud! Did he know 'twas you he kissed that day?"

Carol sighed. Under ordinary circumstances she would never have discussed her private affairs with an abigail, especially Ada, even though she loved her like a relative, but Flossie was different. She was young, just three years her junior, and in the short time she had served her she thought of her more as a friend than a maid. Furthermore, she'd already been indiscreet enough to confide in Flossie back at the inn. She didn't regret it, either, because at the time she needed someone to share her misery and shame. Yes, shame! Because she'd allowed herself to succumb to his demanding kiss, and he knew it! And she believed he was taunting her with that knowledge. Still, she couldn't be absolutely sure. That's why she needed an extra shoulder to carry her humiliating burden. So, sighing again, she said, "I don't know, Flossie. His manners were impeccable, he acted as if we were meeting for the first time, but several things he said could have carried a double meaning. It was his eyes, I think, which unnerved me. They seemed to read my every thought and to laugh at them."

"Oh, ma'am!" Flossie murmured as she followed

her mistress over to the small round table near the window and proceeded to pour hot chocolate from the flowered china pot into a matching china cup. "How awful for you." Suddenly her eyes brightened. "Maybe you're just seeing things that ain't really there. Maybe he really ain't the one. 'Tis possible, aint it?"

Carol sipped the hot milky-sweet liquid. "Maybe so," she conceded, more to please Flossie than for any other reason. The girl seemed genuinely distressed over the incident and Carol, with her innate kindness, wanted to ease that distress. But down in the secret recesses of her heart Carol felt he was the one; yet, clinging to that slender thread of doubt, prayed she was wrong.

It was almost tea time when Flossie came into the drawing room where Carol and Aunt Minnie sat awaiting the tea cart with it silver appointments, the warm tantalizing crumpets and mouth-watering scones. Her face was flushed and her eyes sparkled like dewdrops in the sun.

"Oh, ma'am, look what just came for you! Ain't it lovely?" She handed a nosegay of violets to Carol. "And this note was delivered with it," she added, passing the heavy vellum envelope across to her mistress.

Carol took it into her hands, glanced at the bold handwriting that spelled her name. Instinctively, she knew it was from Overton, but to Aunt Minnie pretended ignorance.

"Oh, I wonder who could have sent it?" She buried her lovely classic nose deep into the sweet-smelling purple blossoms.

"We'll never know, my dear, if you don't open

the note, or did you intend to keep it a mystery?"
Aunt Minnie said, smiling over at her niece. She,
too, suspected the flowers and note were from the
Duke of Overton, but didn't want her suspicions
known, either. Lady Minerva had a feeling that this
Season would be more profitable for Carol than last
year, and to attract the attentions of the most
charming unmarried man in all London at the very
beginning of the Season was indeed a feather in her
cap. Not that she harbored any thoughts of the
duke making an offer for Carol, for she didn't, but
attention from him would very likely bring forth attention from other eligible men, *young* men of rank
and breeding. She still thought the duke was too old
for her niece; besides, she would rather Carol married a man who didn't have such a scandalous past.
Still, it didn't hurt any for the *ton* to see that His
Grace the Duke was interested in Carol. But as she
watched Carol's fingers rip open the envelope, a
nagging thought knitted her brow. Last night at Almack's, Carol had been as cool to the duke as possible without being actually rude. Why? she
wondered. Was the girl daft not to see the advantages in such a friendship?

Of course, it was from the duke, just as she suspected, but rather than hand it over to her aunt, she
read the message aloud. That way Flossie could
hear, too, as Carol could tell she was as anxious as
Aunt Minnie to know what it said.

"My dear Lady Carolyn," the note began.

Please accept this small bouquet as a token of
the great pleasure it was to have made your
acquaintance. It has been a long time since I

have encountered a lady who possessed such charm, such wit, such maidenly modesty as yourself. I fervently hope you will count me as a dear friend among your many others. My mother and sister join me in this hope, and they urge me to request you and your charming aunt to join them in a ride through the park tomorrow afternoon. Their barouche will call at your abode promptly at five o'clock. My groom will await your answer.

Your Obedient Servant
James Farrell, Duke of Overton

By the time she finished reading, Carol's fingers were trembling. It was all she could do to hold them under control so that Aunt Minnie wouldn't guess her feelings. She wanted to crumple the note *and* the nosegay and fling them in his groom's face to be returned to *His Insolent Grace*. The nerve of that man! To an outsider his words were innocuous, but to her they were written in the poisonous ink of sarcasm. She had been neither charming, nor witty, nor, as she had demonstrated in her surprising embrace, possessed of maidenly modesty. How his taunting words infuriated her! But like a rabbit caught in a trap, she couldn't do anything about it. Aunt Minnie would practically swoon if she refused to be friendly with the duke and his family. She'd consider it an affront to *her* prestige.

After a short conversation with her aunt in which she happily agreed to accompany her on the ride, Carol crossed over to the elegantly carved escritoire, sat down, dipped a pen in the standish and wrote her reply. It was polite, short and to the point. She thanked him for the nosegay, said she and Lady Minerva would be happy to accompany Her Grace the Duchess and Lady Laura on a ride through the park, and would be ready when the barouche called for them. She made no mention of his compliments nor that she would consider him a friend. Shaking sand over the inked words, she then folded the paper and gave it to Flossie to give to the waiting groom.

As they partook of their tea, Lady Minerva was all agog over the invitation. She prattled on about what a *coup* Carol had pulled by drawing the duke's attentions and how nice it would be for her to have a young friend so near her own age as the Lady Laura.

Carol only half listened. She, too, thought it would be nice to have Laura for a friend, for she had been very favorably impressed with her last night. She liked the duchess, too. The only thing that troubled her was how she could be a friend to the two women and be forced to be around that black-hearted duke without showing her aversion to him. Well, she'd just have to be a good actress, that's all there was to it. Then, too—and this thought cheered her somewhat—no doubt he'd grow tired of baiting her and find his pleasure elsewhere. Yes, she thought, more than likely that's what will happen. He'll taunt her a few more times then take off for greener pastures. She was almost back to her cheerful self when Flossie came back into the room to inquire what gown should she ready for tomorrow's carriage ride.

Usually Carol wouldn't have paid much notice to

Flossie, just answered her and let it go at that, but something gay and lilting in Flossie's soft voice made her look at her intently. Her face was still flushed and her blue eyes still sparkled as they did when she brought in the duke's flowers and note. At that time, Carol had just supposed it was due to being the bearer of an unaccustomed gift, but now she wondered. Then it struck her!

"Flossie," Carol said, "what sort of groom does the duke have? Is he tall or short? Young or old? Ugly or handsome?"

Flossie ducked her head, her face turning a deeper pink. "Oh, ma'am," she giggled, "how you do go on. Do you think I notice every man what comes along?"

Carol laughed. "I think you notice any young man who notices you, and I have the feeling the duke's groom did just that. Am I right?"

Behind cupped fingers, another giggle escaped from the little maid's throat. "Well, ma'am, he was young, about as tall as Pa, with the reddest hair and bluest eyes I ever saw and more freckles than a dog has fleas. It couldn't rightly be said he was handsome, but he did have the sweetest smile ever and the strangest name. He's called Liam."

"It's quite apparent you hardly noticed him, Flossie, 'tis a pity, too, or you might have told us what he looked like," Lady Minerva said, dryly.

Flossie's blush deepened at Lady Minerva's teasing words and Carol's lilting laugh. "It's all right, dear, we understand, but remember what I told you, I'm responsible for you until I return you to your mother, so don't you be getting into any mischief with every Tom, Dick or Harry that smiles at you."

"Oh, ma'am!" Flossie replied. "I promise you won't have any cause to worry about me." She turned towards the door. "I'll go up right now to make sure your cream Berlin silk is properly pressed for your outing."

As she left the room, Carol smiled at her aunt. "Flossie is a dear little thing. I'm sorry George was so ill that Ada had to remain in Worster with him, but I'm glad Flossie took her place. She is so young, so gay, and so full of spirit. She's absolutely wide-eyed at the vastness of this city."

"I agree," said Lady Minerva, "but I think she bears watching. She's so naive and trusting, she might be easily led down the primrose path."

"Oh, I don't think so, Aunt Minnie. True, she's trusting, but she's sensible, too." Carol picked up her tea cup, made a *moue*. "My tea's cold. I could do with a spot of hot, how about you? Shall I ring for Bridget?"

Lady Minerva agreed that would be nice. When Bridget brought in fresh tea, they began to sip it, giving no more thought to Flossie. Neither of them dreamed that the time would come, and before the Season ended, too, that they would question Flossie's good sense.

Chapter Six

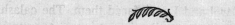

A few minutes before five o'clock on the following
afternoon, a very stylish barouche with the Overton
crest drew up in front of Lady Minerva's Berkeley
Square address. Flossie, who was waiting for it to
appear, ran to get her mistress, and by the time the
footman raised the brass knocker, Lady Minerva
and Lady Carolyn were ready to be escorted to the
carriage.

Carol noticed the splendid pair of matched grays
that pranced in eagerness to be off, appraising them
to be expensive blooded cattle. Little Flossie, left
standing in the doorway as the ladies descended the
outside stone steps, noticed the driver that held the
reins of those spirited horses. It was Liam. And
with the barest of smiles and the almost impercepti-
ble nod of his red-thatched head, he took notice of
her, as well. As surreptitious as Liam tried to make
his awareness of young Flossie, Carol saw it and
was amused. Smothering her smile, she had to
agree with Flossie. He wasn't handsome, but his
coloring and his openness of face with those clear
blue eyes elicited a feeling of trust and kindness.
Yes, Carol thought, Flossie would be safe with this
man, if it ever came to that. She judged him to be

about twenty-four or thereabouts, young, but old enough to be thinking of taking on a wife.

However, she dismissed thoughts of them both as she was handed into the fashionable carriage. The duchess and Lady Laura smiled their welcome, and had arranged for the two older women to sit on one side while Carol and Laura faced them. The calash top was folded down allowing the sun to warm them as the horses pulled them at a spankingly smart clip.

Lady Laura unfurled a dainty blue sunshade that matched her soft voile dress and held it with white kid gloved hands at a most becoming angle. It shaded her porcelain-white complexion, at the same time afforded a full view of her face.

"Don't you fear the sun will spot your face, Lady Carolyn?" she asked, noting that Carol wasn't carrying a parasol.

"Not really. I like to feel its warmth on my skin, but I suppose, for fashion's sake, I ought to carry one." She leaned towards her aunt. "Remind me to carry a parasol the next time we come for a ride, will you?" Then, realizing it must appear as if she took for granted another invitation was forthcoming, quickly said, "That is, of course, if you will accept a ride in our carriage tomorrow. We would love for you both to be our guests. Don't you agree, Aunt Minnie?"

Lady Minerva smiled. "Yes, indeed, but I'm afraid tomorrow is out of the question. I have a fitting at Madame LeBeau's at four o'clock and won't be back in time to ride." She turned to the duchess. "Will the day after tomorrow be convenient for you and Lady Laura?"

The duchess said that she, too, had an engagement for the following afternoon and the day after as well, but she would be glad to accept another invitation in the very near future. Carol bit her lip, thinking she had pushed things a bit too far, but Laura seemed actually glad that neither of the older women could go and suggested that since she and Lady Carolyn were free both afternoons, they might have a carriage ride together.

"I'm sure, Mama, Lady Minerva's coachman and her footmen will be very good chaperones, but if you think we need more, we'll both bring our abigails. Please, Mama, say yes. I dislike to miss an outing just because you'll be busy." And before the duchess could answer, Laura laid a gloved hand on Carol's arm. "You wouldn't like to have to stay home, either, would you?"

Carol had nothing to keep her from going for a ride; but for some reason, she felt even if she had the compelling look in Laura's sapphire eyes would force her to acquiesce. She had the strangest feeling that somehow it was very important to Laura that Carol accompany her on a ride through the park the following day. Of course she agreed, and the arrangements were made. And again she had the feeling Laura was pleased as she smiled and relaxed against the cushioned seat.

Between the hours of five and six on any fine afternoon, it was *de rigueur* for the *ton* to be seen driving, riding, or walking through Hyde Park. And today all of London seemed to be out *en masse*. The drive was so crowded with various types of carriages it was all Liam could do to keep the horses under control enough to stay in line. The walks were crowded with debutantes and their mamas followed by a coterie of eager swains. A few fathers accompanied their daughters, but only a very few. Mostly the males were young men turned out in the latest modes of fashion—high starched collars with piercing points, elaborately wound neckcloths, superbly cut waistcoats and thigh-hugging breeches of excellent superfine. There were a sprinkling of dandies nicknamed macaroni because of their exaggerated articles of clothing such as very high-crowned hats, dangling fobs, and colored high-heeled shoes on which they minced along with affectedly dainty steps.

Also, there were riders, both ladies with their grooms in attendance and gentlemen alone or riding in pairs. Most all of the mounts were fine-looking blooded stock, and their riders, male and female, seemed to be of the same high breeding. Even if one discounted the lovely old trees with their spring-green finery, the flowers that bloomed profusely in all spectra of colors perfuming the air sweetly with their odors, just seeing the people thronging the Park was enjoyable enough.

The duchess and Lady Minerva were deep in conversation about various household subjects as Carol relaxed against the cushions, taking in all the sights and sounds and odors. The carriage was making the second lap around the park when Carol realized Lady Laura was scanning each face as if searching for one in particular. For several minutes she observed her, thinking surely she was mistaken. But no, she was definitely looking for one certain face in that crowd of faces that thronged about them. Whose could it be? Her brother's, the duke's?

Carol certainly hoped it wasn't his, but whose? She supposed it was the duke's. Since this was Laura's very first time to come to London, she knew no one here except those she met at Almack's last night. Could she be searching for one of those on such short acquaintance?

Soon Carol's curiosity was satisfied, but just barely, and if she hadn't been looking at Laura at that precise moment she'd have missed it. A young man on a bay horse came slowly cantering down the path from the opposite direction their carriage traveled. Laura's blue eyes widened, gleamed brightly, and the ghost of a smile played across her lips. Carol quickly looked at the same young man who'd brought such a reaction from Laura, just in time to see an answering gleam in his own eyes. He started to bring up his hand to doff his brown beaver hat, but at a slight shake of Laura's ruffled bonnet quickly brought it down again and passed on by without a sign of recognition.

That's odd, Carol thought. He was definitely not at the Assembly last night, but Laura knew him, had been looking for him, yet gave no hint of it whatsoever. Carol had thought last night that the duke's sister was no ninnyhammer. Now she was further intrigued. As Lady Laura relaxed her vigil and began to concentrate on the scenery around her as if all was well within her, an old adage came to Carol's mind—still waters run deep. Yes, there was definitely more here than met the eye.

When the ride was over and the carriage had drawn up at Lady Minerva's house to drop off Carol and her aunt, and all the amenities had been taken care of, Laura leaned over the side of the barouche and said, "Remember now, Lady Carolyn, we shall ride together tomorrow in your carriage. I shall be ready and eagerly awaiting you." She looked over at the duchess. "Is it really necessary that we take our abigails, Mama? I'm sure Lady Carolyn's coachman and footmen will be sufficient protection." Without waiting for a reply, she turned back to Carol. "Don't you agree that's enough chaperonage?"

She seemed so insistent, and her blue eyes held Carol's own topaz ones so firmly, that Carol didn't dare disagree had she thought differently. So it was arranged that the following afternoon the young ladies would ride in Lady Minerva's smart landau without their abigails and with only Coachman and the footmen as chaperones. As Carol and her aunt made their way into the house and the Overton barouche made its way down the street, Carol was struck again by the ease with which Lady Laura had maneuvered their next outing to her advantage, whatever that might be.

The hour arrived and Coachman stopped in front of the duke's Grosvenor Square town house on time. Lady Laura was ready and waiting and skipped gaily down the steps and into the carriage in high spirits. This time she was dressed in pink silk with another matching parasol and a straw bonnet with a wide pink ribbon tied under her chin and arranged into a charming bow to the side. Carol was dressed in green, a color that brought out the golden flecks of her hazel eyes. And this time she, too, carried a matching parasol. Judging by the admiring looks they received as they drove along the streets and into the park, they made a charming pair.

Though Lady Laura made light conversation with Carol commenting on the various carriages with their fashionable passengers, the riders and pedestrians that passed, Carol had the same impression she had the day before. Laura was searching the crowd for one particular face. And he wasn't long in coming.

Just as it happened yesterday, a lone rider on a bay horse approached them from the opposite direction. Only this time, Lady Laura smiled broadly and gave a small salute with her pink gloved hand. The gentleman doffed his hat and bowed. Then, making sure no other rider was in his way, turned his mount so that he could ride alongside the landau.

"Good afternoon, Lady Laura. What good fortune to find you here in the city. When did you arrive?"

Laura lowered her eyes, her black lashes sweeping her flushed cheeks, and with a smile looked back up at him and said, "About a se'ennight ago, Mr. Lippinscot. And it's a pleasure to see you here, too. Are you in London on business, perchance?"

But before he could reply, Laura's smile widened. "Oh, forgive me my manners. Before becoming so inquisitive, I should have presented to you my very *dear* friend, Lady Carolyn Travis of Worster Hall." Turning to Carol, she said, "And this is The Honorable Roland Lippinscot of Kirkland Park."

Carol smiled and nodded her salutation as the young man on horseback made a sweeping bow with his beaver hat while still managing to keep his prancing mount under control.

Lady Laura turned to Carol again to say, "Mr. Lippinscot and his family live a few miles from Overton Castle. We've known each other since childhood." She cut her blue eyes around to him in mock severity. "Roland was quite a tease as a boy. He used to pull my curls when he thought no one was looking. And it hurt, too!"

"Oh, Lady Laura, I had hoped you'd forgotten such boyish pranks as that. Once again I beg your forgiveness."

Laura's pert little nose lifted upward, her eyes flashed like sapphires and her blond curls swung merrily under the confines of her saucy bonnet. "I'll think about it. And if Lady Carolyn would accompany me, I'd alight from the carriage and walk with you over to where those lovely lilacs are blooming. By that time I'd have made up my mind whether to forgive you or not."

Carol could read between the lines enough to know that what Lady Laura really wanted was a chance to be alone with the handsome brown-haired young man with the sparkling amber eyes and round cherub's face. She wasn't sure it was proper for Laura to walk off with her friend alone, but after all, this was *1812,* not the Dark Ages! Besides, it was broad daylight and she herself would be close by, so, pleading that her satin shoes were unsuitable for walking, Carol urged Laura to go on for the walk while she stayed in the carriage and Coachman slowly circled the park one more time.

Laura feigned dismay that Carol wouldn't accompany her, but at the same time she let the footman help her out while Mr. Lippinscot dismounted and tied his horse to the back of the carriage. With his hand lightly guiding Lady Laura's elbow, they began walking down the path to the lilac bed.

As Coachman drew near to the lilacs after circling the grounds with the extra mount in tow, Mr. Lippinscot halted him with a gesture of his upraised hand, handed Lady Laura back in the landau and told both the young ladies he hoped to meet them again very soon. He untied his horse and with another doff of his hat rode away in the opposite direction.

For a moment or two they rode along in silence, then Laura turned to Carol and said, "Dear Lady Carolyn, I hope you didn't think me too forward when I introduced you as 'my very dear friend,' especially since we only met the other evening, but I do like you and hope we *can* be friends, because I am very much in need of one."

"Of course I didn't mind, Lady Laura. I, too, like you and shall be honored to be your friend." Carol reached over to lightly pat the back of Laura's gloved hand. "Would I be too inquisitive if I asked why you feel so strongly that you need a friend?"

Laura blushed, looked down at her hands whose fingers were busy twisting and twirling the end of her parasol. "I need a friend from whom I can beg a favor."

Carol laughed. "I gather the favor is not to mention you met Mr. Lippinscot today. In that case, you can count on my silence. For that matter, you can be assured I will also say nothing about you seeing him yesterday and signaling him to pass on by unnoticed."

Laura's flushed face darkened, a tiny smile curved her shapely lips. "I didn't think you noticed, but thank goodness Mama didn't see him. I don't want her to know he's in town until after I talk to you. And that brings me to the favor I hope to get from you. I don't know how one gets invited to Almack's, but if you do and can arrange it so that he can go there to the Assemblies, I'd be ever so grateful. That way maybe my brother and my mother could get to know him better and like him enough to let me marry him even though he doesn't have money and property of his own."

Carol was a bit taken aback at such a confession. She also was quite sure the duke would heartily dislike any such meddling on her part to help his sister meet the young man socially.

"Are you in love with The Honorable Mr. Lippinscot, Lady Laura?"

"I-I don't know. I-I-I th-think so. At least, I'd like the opportunity to be around him enough to find out."

"Tell me more about him, dear. Is he of good family connections?"

Lady Laura's eyes brightened a little as she began to answer. "Oh, yes, indeed. His family goes back almost to the Norman Conquest. In fact, Kirkland Park is a very old castle built in the twelfth century. For a long time its owners were very wealthy and titled gentlemen." Her eyes lost some of their glow. "But by the time Roland's father took over, much of the wealth had been dissipated, and what was left Baron Lippinscot gambled away. Not only was the baron a gaming man but also a very—ah—profligate person. He married Roland's mother only for her inheritance and went through that as quickly as he did his own."

Laura dabbed at her moist eyes with a lace handkerchief before continuing. "Lady Lippinscot is a very unhappy person. 'Tis most sad to see how dreary her life is, especially since the baron's suicide and the resulting scandal. Fortunately, the baron's sister was the widow of Lord Craddock by that time and had enough money to pay up all his debts and save Kirkland Park from being taken out of family hands. She saw to it that Roland and his mother and sister were able to live in ease and that Roland was given an education. Even now, his sister is still with a tutor at home."

"If the aunt has done all that, why won't she provide for Mr. Lippinscot to get married?"

Laura sighed. "Well, that's another story and one I really don't know completely. Roland told me a little bit of it, but said he was a victim of circumstance more than of guilt. It seems when he was about seventeen or eighteen there was some to-do about one of the servant girls getting into trouble and claiming Roland was responsible. He denied it, but his aunt believed the girl rather than him. She vowed when he finished his education he would get nothing more from her. From then on, he was on his own. She changed her will, fixing it so that Dorothy, Roland's sister, would inherit Kirkland Park and the Craddock estate and wealth in the event of her marriage, provided she married with the blessing of her mother and aunt. Otherwise, both estates would go to the upkeep and care of orphans. Since there are no Craddock heirs left living, it was perfectly legal for Lady Craddock to do this.

"She cut him off completely over a boyish misdemeanor, and one of which he may not even be guilty? She must be a very vicious person," commented Carol.

"In a way, she is. She's very generous with her niece and sister-in-law, but she never liked her brother and she sees traits in Roland that she thinks are like the baron's. She says she doesn't want Kirkland Park to ever again be in danger of being sold to pay gaming debts or as a result of mismanagement." Laura turned to face Carol, grasped one of her hands in hers. "But, Roland's not at all like his father. He's kind and thoughtful and moral. Please, believe me, he's really a very nice young man."

For a fleeting moment Carol thought of the fortune-hunter who had made her last Season so disastrous. Was The Honorable Mr. Lippinscot of that stripe, too? Also, she thought once again of how much the duke would dislike her aiding and abetting his sister in pursuing a friendship with young Lippinscot, for she had no doubt that he was aware of the man's family history and penniless state. Yet, she was moved to pity by Laura's pretty face so crestfallen and sad at the thought of not being able to see her friend at social functions. Another wicked little thought entered her mind. By helping Laura, she would be getting a bit of revenge on the arrogant Duke of Overton for the high-handed way he had treated her. She'd do it! Edward could get a voucher to Almack's for Mr. Lippinscot. She'd ask him this very day.

Another disturbing thought popped to mind. Edward seemed smitten with the Lady Laura himself. Would he want to do anything to encourage competition? Knowing her brother's pride, she decided to play upon it. If he refused and young Roland wasn't allowed to see Laura, she would always think of him as her lost love. If Roland was underfoot, Laura would have the chance to compare him with a mature man like Edward and would see for herself that he paled in comparison. Yes, that's the tack she'd use, and she was sure it would succeed.

Covering Laura's clutching fingers with her own, she said, "I'll do what I can, Lady Laura. I should know if I'm successful in a day or two. Meantime, don't worry. I'm sure things will work out to your advantage."

The blue eyes widened and sparkled, the shapely mouth curved into a smile. "Oh, Lady Carolyn, I just knew I could place my trust in you. How can I ever thank you enough?"

Carol laughed. "Well, to begin, let's drop the formality. Since we're practically the same age, why not call me 'Carol' as my family does instead of 'Lady Carolyn?' "

"I'd like that. And you can call me 'Lolly,' as *my* family does. Truth to tell, I'm really not quite used to 'Lady Laura' as yet, anyway."

They laughed together and their friendship was cemented. The bond between them would harden and stay firm throughout a lifetime.

Chapter Seven

Viscount Lynsford did procure the voucher for The Honorable Roland Lippinscot, and for the last several Assemblies he was a very welcome addition. He was charming to all the ladies—young, elderly and in between. He was an excellent dancer, a witty supper companion and as much liked by the men guests as by the women. As an attractive extra man, he was rapidly being included in all the invitation lists other than Almack's. Wherever Lady Carolyn and Lady Laura went, there he was; also. He shared the private dinner parties, the routs, drums, balls, even an opera box with Lady Laura and the duchess.

For Lady Carolyn this Season was much different from last year's. Being singled out by the Duke of Overton had a great deal to do with it, Carol knew, but that wasn't the whole reason. She, herself, was different. Less shy, more discreet in the way she handled herself with the various young men who buzzed around her like so many bees sipping honey. She didn't blurt out her opinions nearly so often, especially when they differed from the men's, and when she did express herself, she was more subtle and pleasant. She credited Lolly with showing her how to better please both the men and the women, how to smile enigmatically and lower and raise her lashes at the proper time. Whatever made this Season a success, she had no lack of invitations and no lack of gentlemen from whom to chose escorts. However, no matter who asked to be her escort, she almost invariably chose either her brother or her cousin. The one thing she hadn't learned was complete trust. With Edward or Troy she knew she wasn't being escorted for her money. Then, too, she enjoyed a certain amount of freedom to converse or dance with whomever she pleased without raising anyone's eyebrows. One escort she never chose was the Duke of Overton, and for a very good reason. He never asked her! But he showered her with attentions in other ways. Hardly a day went by that a little nosegay, or a single rose, or a small bouquet wasn't delivered by Liam to the Berkeley Square house. Sometimes these little gifts were accompanied by a verse or two, sometimes by just his signature.

These attentions puzzled her. She still thought of the duke as an odious man, and yet—and yet, she caught herself looking forward to the deliveries Liam made with pleasure. At the same time, she'd recall the high-handed way he treated her that day at the inn and her resentment always returned. She still wasn't sure he connected her with that barefooted girl he had kissed because not once had he admitted it to her. However, from time to time some of his words were veiled in such a way that they could be taken at face value or with hidden references to that meeting. With all the attentions he showered upon her—the hand-delivered gifts, the charming way he treated her at the various social functions they both attended—it nettled her that he never asked to escort her personally. Actually, she wished he would, just so she could refuse. Another thing that galled her was that he seemed to realize this, and so never gave her the chance. But the thing that bothered her the most was the fact that, as they danced or chatted together whenever they met socially, she found him so charming she felt herself slipping under his spell in spite of all she could do.

One person had no such problem. Flossie was delighted with the duke's delivered gifts because their arrival always gave her and Liam a chance to meet and have a little tête-à-tête, and she was quite open in her pleasure. To prolong their little visits, Carol always had Liam wait until she could pen her thanks to the duke in a little note which he could take back with him. It amused her to see the warm and friendly glances the two servants exchanged and the scowl that Groom Tim wore whenever Liam appeared.

By now Carol and Lolly were fast friends, almost like sisters. They shared many girlish secrets together and had their private moments of imitating some of the stiff-necked Patronesses and other matronly social leaders, collapsing in peals of laughter together. The only secret Carol didn't share with Lolly was her feeling about the duke. In fact, she tried to avoid all mention of him whenever they conversed. She didn't want to say anything unpleasant about Lolly's brother, and she didn't want to be placed in a position where she was forced to praise him, either.

She got along swimmingly with the duchess, too. They both had one love in common—their pedigreed little Yorkshire terriers. Carol had described her little pet, Imp, to the duchess and the duchess in turn presented her own little pet—a female, formally named Queen Guinevere, informally called Guinny. They made plans to breed them at some future time and share whatever litter was produced.

But it wasn't until the Newtons's masquerade party that Carol discovered how bitterly opposed Overton was to Mr. Roland Lippinscot's voucher to Almack's, and how displeased he was with her over her part in securing it.

As usual, Edward was escorting Lolly to the masquerade. Lolly was very careful not to accept direct invitations from Mr. Lippinscot for fear her brother and mother would get suspicious and see that she was favoring him above all the other young men who clamored for her attentions. She felt safe with Viscount Lynsford and let him escort her more than any of the others. However, once arrived at whichever social function she attended, Lolly made sure she spent a satisfactory time with Mr. Lippinscot.

Carol knew of Lolly's little ruse and was sure Edward did, too, but the fact that he was Lolly's favorite escort encouraged him enough to compete with Mr. Lippinscot for as much of her attention as he could get. At least, he told Carol, Lolly enjoyed his company and made no bones about showing it. Still, it bothered Carol, because she could see Edward was very close to falling in love with Lolly. If he lost out, she knew he would be deeply hurt.

Troy Ravenhill also tried to secure as much of Lady Laura's time as possible, but didn't have much luck. Overton seemed to always manage to be near enough to his sister whenever Troy was around to cast a damper on his advances. The duke wasn't overtly antagonistic to Troy, but in subtle ways let it be known he didn't approve of him as a suitor for his sister's hand. And Lord Ravenhill was bitterly aware of this.

Carol, also, was aware of this tug-o'-war between the two men. She wondered why. The duke accepted her brother's attentions to Lolly, why not her cousin's? After all, they were both from the same respectable family.

But, back to the masquerade party. Edward's barouche bringing Lolly and the duchess arrived in front of the Newtons's at the same time Troy's landau halted with its passengers—Lady Carolyn, Lady Minerva and Lady Katherine.

Each group greeted the other with smiles and nods and, between Carol and Lolly, gay giggles of pleasure and admiring comments on their attire. The girls did look lovely. Lolly was a dream in a soft powder blue domino, a matching loo-mask dangling by its strings from her fingers ready to be donned prior to entering the Newtons's large graystone house. Her blond curls were arranged in the stylish *Méduse* and her blue eyes flashed like sapphires.

Carol was equally as charming in a shimmering rose-colored domino and loo-mask, her thick mane of shining chestnut hair dressed *à la diadème*.

Aunt Minnie and Cousin Kate were appropriately gowned as befitted their matronly status. Lady

Minerva in amethyst sarsnet and Lady Katherine in her standard gray brocade, a gown she wore to nearly every large affair. It worried Carol that Cousin Kate had such a paucity of suitable gowns. Surely, with all the wealth from his estate, Troy could well afford for his mother to dress on a scale worthy of his rank. But when she looked over to where Lord Ravenhill was handing over the reins of the landau to the Newtons's groom, she was even more puzzled. Troy was well-attired in a fashionable suit of black superfine, a snowy white neckcloth wound around his neck in the stylish and intricate manner known as the Mathematical Tie. But what puzzled her was realizing he, too, had worn the same outfit as often as Cousin Kate had worn her brocade. Did they just not care for new clothes, or was Troy monstrously in the wind? And for what reason? She could think of nothing that would require so much of his money that he wouldn't have enough to spend on such luxuries as new clothes for himself and his mother. Edward's income was a trifle smaller than Troy's, but he managed beautifully. She just didn't understand it at all.

However, once inside the Newtons's house, Carol forgot all about Lord Ravenhill's monetary affairs and gave herself over to admiring the spacious residence. There seemed to be a million candles casting a soft suffusion of light over the entire party—furniture, decorations, people, everything. It was like a rosy-hued fairyland. At one corner of the ballroom, a string ensemble was tuning up for a minuet. At the other end, white-coated servants were waiting to serve the icy punch that sparkled in huge cut-glass bowls. Everyone wore their loo-masks, but it wasn't hard to distinguish who was who. Close by the raised platform that held the musicians sat the Marchioness of Cromart Court with her dull-eyed obese daughter, Leah, in tow. Carol thought it was sad that even with all her money Leah didn't stand much chance of snaring a suitable husband. Then there were the usual group of young men who were variously described as Pinks or Corinthians or Exquisites as well as a sprinkling of those who were recognized as rich ne'er-do-wells, fortune-hunters, and even a few rake-shames. But generally the crowd was made up of the *haut ton,* the mothers and fathers of mar-riageable daughters all seeking eligible suitors as prospective husbands for their offsprings, and en-joying themselves in the pursuit.

Even the renowned Mr. George Bryan Brum-mell, more widely known as Beau Brummell, was there. Carol had met the great Society leader and bosom friend of the Prince Regent last Season, but it was only this Season, and then only after the Duke of Overton had claimed so many of her waltzes, that the eminent Mr. Brummell conde-scended to invite her to dance with him. She was prepared to dislike him. She considered him an ego-centric person. In spite of herself, she warmed to him. He was handsome in a dashing manner, a great wit, and a very amiable person, if one hap-pened to win his favor. But heaven help those who incurred his disfavor! He could make or break a person's reputation with a single well-aimed jest. To be the recipient of his charms was to be the envy of every female in the *ton*. Carol didn't give his attentions too much thought, but her Aunt Minnie breathed much easier when he showed that Lady Carolyn was in his circle of favored ones.

One person was conspicuous by his absence, the Duke of Overton. Carol scanned each face as she danced and whirled around the ballroom, but she didn't see him. Later, when she and Lolly chanced to meet near the refreshment table while their current dancing partners were getting them cups of punch, she casually asked if the duke intended coming to the party. As soon as the question was out, she wondered why she had asked it. What did she care if he came or not? But for some reason, she did care, and she couldn't explain it had she tried.

"Yes, I think so," Lolly answered. "He mentioned having to go someplace else first, but promised to be here before the midnight unmasking time."

When their escorts arrived with the cups of punch and they had partaken of a sip or two, Lolly turned to her young man and said, "Would you kindly excuse me? I have a slight headache and think I'll go upstairs to lie down for a bit."

The young man became very solicitous, asking if he should ask the duchess to accompany her.

"Oh, no!" Lolly said quickly. "It's not that serious. I wouldn't want her to worry about me. Besides, Lady Carolyn will accompany me, won't you, dear?"

Carol tried to hide her surprise and quickly replied that certainly she would go with her upstairs. She excused herself from her dancing partner, and the two of them moved towards the stairs. As the men disappeared from view, Lolly stopped, gave a small signal with her hand towards a large potted palm near the stairwell and who should pop into view from behind the fronded greenery but Roland Lippinscot!

Lolly grinned at Carol. "I've changed my mind again. I think I'll go out on the terrace. The fresh air will do my "headache" much more good than lying down, don't you agree?"

Carol returned her grin. "Oh, Lolly! You *are* a minx! I just pray you don't get caught in your own tangled web."

"What I wish is that we were at the ridotto at Ranelagh. I'm sure it's much livelier than this party." She turned to Roland. "Will you escort me there sometime soon?"

"Indeed I will not," Mr. Lippinscot replied. "You know public ridottos are looked upon as vulgar affairs, and your brother would have my scalp if I escorted you to one."

"Fie on my brother!" she said, pouting her pretty mouth. With a quick smile, she placed her hand on his arm and the two of them walked towards the lantern-festooned terrace.

Not wanting to stand there alone, Carol decided to go out on the terrace, too. There were many shrubs that grew around the stone appendage that cast deep shadows in which she could hide herself from view of the strolling couples that paraded up and down seeking a bit of relief from the strenous dancing. That way, she too could catch a breath of fresh air without being thought of as a wallflower. But as she blended herself in the dark shadow of a large stone column as well as that of a huge Ligustrum bush, she caught more than fresh air. She overheard a conversation she was sure was not intended for her ears.

Just as she wedged herself between the large column and the overhanging boughs of the giant shrubbery, she heard footsteps approach and stop just before reaching the stone column. A male voice she recognized as Mr. Brummell's said, "Well, Overton, I see you finally showed up. Come to keep an eye on that pretty little sister of yours, or on Lord Worster's young filly?"

The duke laughed softly, and in Carol's mind's eye she could see those sparkling jet eyes. "To be honest, Beau, I guess I've come to see them both. They're both easy on the eyes, don't you agree?"

"That I do, James, that I do."

Carol wished she was anyplace but where she was; however, there was just no way she could leave without being seen, and she certainly didn't want that. But at Mr. Brummell's next question her curiosity was so piqued wild horses couldn't have dragged her away.

"I've watched you at Almack's and some of the private parties paying a great deal of attention to the Lady Carolyn. Tell me, James, are you hanging out for a wife after all?"

"Lud, no!" Overton said. "You know I never intend to marry again. I'll say this, though. If I did, I don't think I could do any better than her. She's a lovely lass."

"Then why all the attentions? Don't you know you're raising the hopes of all the mamas?"

The duke gave a small sigh. "It's a sad story, Beau, and one of which I'm not at all proud. On the way to London at the beginning of the Season I stopped at The Blue Goose Inn. While my horses rested, I decided to take a walk. I met Lady Carolyn and through stupidity, mistook her for a local lass, thought she might even be a barmaid at the inn. Anyway, I didn't act the gentleman, I'm sorry to say, and—well, when I met her at Almack's and realized who she was, I felt as cheap as a clipped farthing. In my way, I've been trying to make up for my boorish behavior."

"Didn't she accept your apology?"

"That's the trouble, I didn't make one. I was almost afraid to do so. Instead, I tried to act as if I didn't recognize her, teased her along in hopes of winning her friendship so that when I do acknowledge my mistake and offer an apology, she'll accept it and see the humorous side of the whole affair."

"And if she doesn't?"

"I don't intend to throw myself off the parapet of the keep at Overton Castle, if that's what you want to know, but I will feel badly if she doesn't. I hope it won't end that way."

Carol's mind was a whirlpool of emotion. Anger, humiliation, a sense of the ridiculousness of the whole situation, plus a soupçon of something she couldn't quite identify turned her brain into a whirling carrousel. Part of her wanted to rush out and confront the duke, another part of her wanted to melt into the shadows and never have to see him again. While this battle waged within her, she heard Mr. Brummell say, "Well, James, I wish you luck, but I've got to go put in another promised appearance. Will you join me?"

"I think not, Beau, not just yet, anyway. I believe I'll indulge in a cigarillo before going in."

From between the flat Ligustrum leaves, Carol watched as Mr. Brummell made his way down the terrace towards the open french doors. A second or so later, she heard the scratch of a match, saw a small burst of flame, then a curl of gray smoke drifted upward and over the shrubbery to fade into the night air. At that moment her battle ended and anger emerged victorious. Pushing aside the pliant green branches, she stepped away from her hiding place and in a stern tone said, "Your Grace, I will have a word with you."

He jerked around, the paper lantern overhead showing the surprise in his dark eyes. "Why, Lady Carolyn! You startled me. I didn't hear you approach. Are you alone?"

"Yes, and I didn't just walk up. I was standing in the shadows on the other side of this column."

With a flip of his finger, he sent the cigarillo arcing into the air. The surprised look left his eyes, wariness took its place. "Oh? Then I take it you eavesdropped on my conversation with Mr. Brummell."

"Not intentionally, I assure you, but when I heard my name bandied about, yes, I listened, and a good thing, too. I've long thought you were aware I was the girl you insulted at The Blue Goose Inn, but until tonight I wasn't absolutely sure. I never dreamed it was cowardice that kept you from begging my pardon. Now, I can add *that* to the long list of your other flaws."

He stepped closer, looked down at her, his lean face grim and his eyes as dark and as hard as obsidian. "I thought you had a better sense of humor than you apparently have and would see that no real harm was done to you. I shouldn't have acted the way I did whether you were a servant girl or of the nobility, but you looked so young, so pretty, such a delicious little morsel, I momentarily forgot to be a gentleman. Instead, I was just a *man* admiring a *maiden*. But since you demand an apology, you'll get one." He placed an arm across his waist, bowed, and mockingly said, "A thousand pardons, my lady, I'm very sorry I kissed you. Be assured your virtuous lips shall never again be sullied by mine." He straightened up, glared at her, his thin nostrils flaring in anger. "In fact, I could say I'm sorry I ever met you, especially after the meddling you've done in my family affairs."

At each stabbing word, Carol flinched inside as if from body blows, but at his last accusation, she was quite taken back, all his sarcasm fading away in her astonishment. "Meddling? Whatever do you mean?"

"I mean that it was you who had the unmitigated gall to secure a voucher so that whippersnapper Lippinscot could go to Almack's and from there ingratiate himself with other hostesses who were addlepated enough to be taken in by his so-called charm. That's what I mean by meddling, my dear Lady Carolyn." He paused long enough to take a deep breath, then continued. "I've known young Roland all his life, and if I had wanted him to direct his addresses toward my sister, I would have seen to it he went to all the right places. But as it is, I have no intention, in spite of you and Lady

Laura, of permitting that fortune-hunter to worm his way into my family. Do I make myself clear?"

Overton looked so fierce and sounded so gruff that Carol forgot her own anger and was on the verge of being afraid. All her former thoughts of revenge disappeared like mist in sunlight. Underneath that well-tailored formal attire was a frame worthy of a pugilist, and his deep voice which was so adept at dulcet badinage was now harsh, unyielding. He is a most puissant man, she thought to herself, and it could be dangerous to provoke him too far. She didn't speak for a moment, then said, her lower lip quivering just a bit. "I apologize, Your Grace. I meant no harm. I just did it to please Lolly."

His grim expression softened somewhat, his tone of voice became less harsh. "She's almost as addle-pated as the rest, but she's young, and I intend to see she outgrows her infatuation for this hare-brained popinjay." He looked out into space a moment, then back at Carol. "And I suppose I shouldn't have railed out at you just for trying to be a friend to my sister."

"Does that mean I can still be friends with Lolly?" Carol asked, timorously.

Suddenly, he smiled, its warmth chasing away all traces of his anger. "Yes, of course, it does. She and my mother like you very much." He cocked his head to one side as a slight breeze lifted a lock of his black hair, then let it fall back across his forehead boyishly. "I like you, too, Lady Carolyn, and hope we can be friends from now on. Can you forget our angry words of a moment ago and let that be a possibility?"

Carol looked at him in silence a long time, her

brain whirling with conflicting thoughts. Finally, she said, "Since we shall most likely be attending the same social functions, I shall be happy to dance with you and converse with you, but since I have your own word that you don't contemplate another marriage, and since I'd refuse an offer from you in the event you might change your mind and make one, I see no future in our becoming friends. After all, that's what this seasonal charade is all about, is it not? So marriageable girls can be displayed before eligible suitors. In that case, we'd both be wasting our time. Furthermore, I suggest your gifts of flowers cease. I don't know why you ever bothered to send them in the first place, but I'm sure you can find a better use for them than sending them to me."

There! she thought, that ought to take care of that! We can behave in public the same as always. I won't have to explain to any of my family or his that anything is wrong between us and I won't be bothered by any private thoughts of him anymore, either.

His smile faded, a cool languid look masked his face. Shrugging his broad shoulders, he said, "Consider it done, my dear, consider it done. I shan't invade your life anymore and I trust you won't meddle in mine again." With that, he turned and walked away.

Carol stood there leaning against the cool stone column for a long time. She had finally told him off, the odious man, but for some unfathomable reason she wasn't nearly so pleased with herself as she thought she'd be. The taste of victory was more like wormwood than honey.

Chapter Eight

It was one of those mid-spring mornings when rain clouds roiled overhead threatening to spill their watery cargoes momentarily. The air was warm, humid, still. Flossie, behind Carol, brought the hairbrush too far forward and its bristles lightly touched her forehead, then as it made its way down the long thick tresses, hit a tangle. Carol snatched the brush from Flossie, saying, "Here, give me that! If you can't brush my hair without scraping my forehead and pulling my hair out by the roots, I'll do it." She began running the silver-backed brush through her hair as if she were currying a horse's mane. Flossie's lower lip trembled a bit, but she managed to say,

"I'm sorry, ma'am, I'll try to be more gentle."

Carol handed the brush back to the little maid. "Well, see that you do. And the chocolate you brought up this morning was almost cold. You know I like it hot and steamy, not luke warm. Another thing, my toast didn't have enough butter on it. In the future, pay more attention to your duties. For the last several days you've acted as if your mind had departed to parts unknown."

Flossie's lips clamped together tightly, her

dimpled chin quivering in spite of all she could do to maintain control. She wanted to tell her mistress that she, too, had not acted like herself lately. She'd found fault with every little thing and been as cross as a bear. But, of course, she said nothing, just brushed the shining chestnut hair as easy as possible. But the straw that broke the camel's back, as the saying goes, was when Carol looked in the mirror at the finished hair arrangement.

"What *is* the matter with you? That's the worst coiffure you've ever done. Are you deliberately trying to make me unattractive?" With that, she reached up, began pulling all the hairpins out, completely undoing all the work Flossie had done.

Flossie couldn't help herself. She clapped a hand over her mouth trying to stifle her sobs, but she wasn't entirely successful. Her little cry of dismay escaped and her tears overflowed at the same time. Turning, she ran out of the room straight into the person of Lady Minerva, who had just stepped through the open bedroom door.

Muttering a muffled "Excuse me, ma'am," Flossie dodged around Lady Minerva's portly figure and disappeared down the hall.

"Well! What's the matter with her?" Lady Minerva asked. "Did you beat her?"

"No, of course not, Aunt Minnie," Carol said with a sigh. "And the question that should have been asked is what's the matter with *me*. I—I—was cross with Flossie. I hurt her feelings." She ran both hands through her loose hair. "I don't know what's come over me lately. I've been surly and ill-tempered and found fault with everything Flossie did. I'm quite ashamed of myself, and I shall tell Flossie so when she's calmed down a bit." She made herself smile. "Sit down, Aunt Minnie, I assure you I won't find fault with you."

Aunt Minnie looked at her niece with narrowed eyes.

"Does the absence of flower deliveries from the Duke of Overton have anything to do with your ill temper?"

So she *had* noticed, after all, Carol thought to herself. She was hoping she wouldn't have to explain anything about the deliveries because one thing would lead to another, and of all people, she didn't want her aunt to know about her encounter with the duke at the inn or at the masquerade party. Stumbling around for the right words, Carol finally said, "The flowers from the duke? Why, I hadn't noticed, but now that you mention it, it *has* been several days since any have arrived. No doubt he grew tired of sending them, or perhaps he's out of town and forgot to make arrangements for their delivery. Anyway, why should they affect me one way or the other? It's more likely this spell of humid weather we've been having lately that's made me cross. Humidity does that to people, I'm told." She laughed. "It certainly couldn't be the absence *or* the presence of those silly little flowers and verses from His Arrogant Grace the Duke of Overton."

Her aunt bit back her words. She wanted to say she thought the lady did protest too much, but wisely, she kept her counsel. At the first of the Season, she only thought the attentions of the duke would draw the attention of other young men to her niece, but lately she'd changed her mind. In spite of the difference in their ages, she had begun to hope the duke himself might make an offer for Carol. After all, fifteen years wasn't really such a large age-span, and a mature man might make Carol a better husband than one nearer her own age. She hoped her niece hadn't done anything foolish to incur the wrath of such a powerful personage as the duke, or even something that would cool his attentions towards her. She'd say no more. She'd bide her time and keep her eyes open for further evidence of how things stood between Carol and Overton. But she felt compelled to ask one more question.

"You like the duke, don't you, Carol? You don't *really* think he's more arrogant than any of the other men you've met this Season?"

Carol laughed, a gay little sound. "I suppose not. All men, especially the rich and titled ones, seem to think they're placed here just for the benefit of all females. And yes, I like Overton, not anymore nor any less than the other men. Now, let's change the subject. Did you want to see me about something special?"

"Yes. I came to tell you Troy's groom brought a note a few minutes ago to tell you to be ready promptly at seven o'clock. He wants to allow plenty of time to drive down Tottenham Road to the Regency Theatre and to be in his box well before the curtain rises. He stresses that he doesn't want to miss even a minute of the performance."

"Is he waiting for an answer?"

"No, I told him we'd both be ready on time and sent him on his way."

"Thank you," Carol said, going over to the heavily carved armoire and throwing open the door. "Troy seems to be quite charmed by this new French actress who plays Desdemona to Othello. And he is very eager for me to see her act, to get my opinion on her ability, so I suppose I should select a proper gown for such a great occasion. What do you plan to wear?" she asked, then gesturing towards the hanging garments, said, "Which one of these should I wear?"

"I plan to wear my amethyst sarsnet. I've never worn it to the theatre before and I plan to get my money's worth out of it. I had to pay Madame LeBeau enough to make it," Lady Minerva said, eyeing her niece with an appraising glance. "And I think you should wear your bronze Italian taffeta. It brings out the golden highlights in your eyes and emphasizes the titian in your hair." She pursed her lips in thought. "I know what will be the perfect coup de grace, my diamond and emerald necklace!" She started out of the room, calling back over her shoulder, "I'll go fetch it right now."

When she returned holding the piece of jewelry, Carol's eyes went wide with pleasure. The necklace was an heirloom of the Simms family and quite the most elegant thing imaginable.

"Oh, Aunt Minnie!" Carol cried, "How very sweet of you to let me wear such a gorgeous thing. Why, I'll outshine every female at the theatre!"

Lady Minerva smiled. "It is a beautiful necklace. I wish my own daughter had lived long enough to have worn it. But Carol, my dear, I think of you as a daughter, too, and it gives me much pleasure to offer you something like this to wear."

Niece and aunt clasped hands, looked at each

other mutely, their eyes conveying their love, then Lady Minerva left the room.

After Carol was left alone, she thought about her crossness to little Flossie, about Aunt Minnie wanting to know if the absence of the duke's flowers had anything to do with her acid disposition. Did it? She wondered herself. She admitted she had missed the little gifts and she was puzzled. She thought once she'd told the duke to cease sending them, she'd be rid of even thinking about him. It hadn't worked that way. It seemed he crowded her thoughts more than ever. For no reason, she caught herself thinking about that day behind The Blue Goose Inn and the kiss he gave her. She felt she had been insulted, at the same time, tiny ripples of—of—could she dare call it pleasure?—washed over her at the way his strong embrace and firm warm lips had made her feel. Even when Aunt Minnie talked about the golden highlights of her eyes, she thought of him. In her mind she could still hear his deep voice softly calling her "Golden Eyes." She got up from her chair, smoothed the skirt of her calico morning dress, shook her head as if to clear out the cobweb of tangled thoughts and pulled the bellcord to summon Flossie.

Flossie's face was tear-stained, but composed when she entered her mistress's room. "You rang, ma'am?" Her voice was cool, quite formal.

"Yes." Carol walked to within inches of where Flossie stood. Taking one of the little maid's hands in hers, she said,

"Flossie, dear, I want to apologize for being so nasty-tempered. I don't know what came over me. This humid, muggy weather, I suppose. Please forgive me. I promise never to hurt your feelings again."

Flossie's eyes became watery again, only this time with relief. "Oh, ma'am, don't give it another thought. I've been edgy, too. I guess we can both blame it on the weather."

"And we'll both try to forget that ugly little scene that took place earlier." Carol smiled. "Now, I'm going to answer Papa's latest letter, the one in which he said that your father was ever so much better, even able to spend half a day at the stables, and looking forward to gaining enough strength to resume his full duties. I'll tell him how pleased you were to hear that. While I'm doing that, you see that my bronze taffeta dress with the matching satin slippers are ready for me to wear tonight."

Flossie's blue eyes gleamed, her mouth split into a wide grin. "Yes, ma'am! I'll be happy to see to that."

As Flossie crossed over to the large *armoire*, Carol said, teasingly, "Shall I also tell your mum you've got a beau on the string named Liam?"

Flossie looked around quickly, a faint blush staining her apple-blossom cheeks. "Oh, ma'am! Don't tell her that!" She lowered her eyes, smiled shyly, "At least, not yet. Wait a bit before mentioning him."

Carol laughed. "All right, I'll wait, but I wager it won't be much longer before his name will be mentioned quite frequently."

As Flossie buried her head among the clothes in the *armoire*, Carol heard a faint giggle coming from that direction.

At seven sharp, Lady Minerva and Lady Carolyn were ready to receive Lord Ravenhill. All the way to the theatre, Troy filled their ears with praise for the beauty and ability of Mlle. Jeanne Dubois, the actress. He was still at it, more or less, when the curtain rose on the first act.

At intermission, Carol was inclined to agree with him. She was indeed a beautiful woman. A Juno-esque brunette with flawless skin and perfect facial bones, a generous mouth that was firm and shapely, and a beautifully husky voice that carried clear up to the rafters. Her acting ability was superb. The minute she stepped on stage, she *was* Desdemona, as if she had been reincarnated to the part. Carol was thrilled by it all—the decor of the theatre, the play itself, and the people who made up the audience. As the houselights went up and she could see clearly, she looked about at the fashionable men and women enjoying it all. But one thing she saw took the edge off her enjoyment.

In the box on the opposite side of the theatre, she saw the Duke of Overton and a lady companion. Lifting her opera glasses, she looked at their faces. The duke, admirably attired in a maroon evening coat and matching breeches, smiled charmingly at the lady to his side. She, in turn, looked up into his eyes with the same kind of smile. Automatically, Carol knew these two were not strangers to each other. There was a quality in their smiles that hinted at an intimacy that was more than just between friends. Again she was puzzled at her reaction. She didn't care who Overton escorted or how well-acquainted he was with any lady. Why, then, this tiny stab of—of—it galled her to even think it might be—jealousy? No matter, she was compelled to know the lady's name.

While Lady Minerva was engaged in conversattion with a friend in the adjoining box, she asked Troy about the duke's companion.

As he handed back the opera glasses, he said, "Oh, that's Lady Diane Netherton, young wife to old Baron Netherton. The duke squires her about quite often. Guess he feels safe with her. She's no threat to his unmarried state, and the old baron is too old to care where his wife goes or with whom." He laughed. "In the first year of their marriage Lady Diane produced an heir, and that was all the Baron wanted from her. She, in turn, acquired access to his fortune, which was what she wanted from him. Now, she flits from party to party while he sits at home nursing his dyspepsia. It's a perfect arrangement. I hope to do as well some day."

"Why, Troy! I'm ashamed of you," Carol said, tapping him sharply on the arm with her fan. Then she smiled. "Oh, you're just teasing me. You wouldn't make such a marriage of convenience as that, I'm sure."

He grinned enigmatically. "Don't be too sure, Cousin, you may not know me as well as you think you do."

Before she could answer, the lights dimmed and the curtain went up on the last act. However, her concentration wasn't as intense as it had been. Her thoughts alternated between wondering just how friendly was the bond between the duke and Lady Diane and if Troy was really serious about wanting to marry for money more than for love. Was that the reason he tried to address himself to Lolly?

And was it for the same reason the duke wouldn't permit him to do so?

She was still mulling these thoughts over in her mind the following morning when Flossie came running into her room, her blue eyes aglow and bearing a single red rose in her hand.

"Ma'am! Look what just came." She handed the rose to her mistress. "And this note came with it, here," she said, reaching into the pocket of her apron and handing over a sealed envelope.

"I suppose it's from the duke and Liam delivered them," Carol said, trying to act nonchalant.

"Yes, ma'am, it is, and he did. Shall I tell him to wait for an answer?" Flossie asked, expectantly.

"Yes, you may, Flossie, and while he waits, it might be nice to offer him some of those fresh scones I smell baking. Do you think Liam would like that?"

Flossie grinned. "I collect he would indeed, ma'am. Thank you. I'll see to it right away. As she turned around the doorpost, Carol saw a flash of white petticoats, the heels of her black slippers as she hurried back to Liam.

With trembling fingers, Carol ripped open the note. She read it a second time to be sure she was seeing it right. It was so out of character, she could hardly believe her eyes.

"My dear Lady Carolyn," the Duke wrote. "It was brought to my attention by my sister that the reason my groom has been so surly and ill-tempered the last several days is because there's been no deliveries at the Berkeley Square house. It seems he's infatuated with your young abigail, Flossie.

"Now, far be it from me to thwart the blossoming of young love by any action of mine. So, in spite of your request that the flowers cease being delivered, I must overrule you for Liam's and Flossie's sake. If you do not want the gifts, feel free to give them to your maid. I'm sure she'll appreciate the gesture.

"I saw you at the theatre last night and wish to compliment you on your appearance. You looked ravishing. Sorry I can't say as much for your escort. I feel sure you can do far better than Lord Ravenhill."

Your Obedient Servant,
James, Duke of Overton

Carol was so surprised it took her a moment or two to react. Then anger came to the fore. The nerve of that man! Criticizing Lord Ravenhill when he knew full well he was her cousin! Only a third cousin, to be sure, still he *was* family. How dare he do such a thing! And he a cicisbeo to Lady Diane Netherton. Oh, really! she thought, he is a most *odious* man.

A few minutes later, she began to smile. It wasn't like the duke to send flowers just to please his groom or her maid. There was more to it than that. Either, Lolly or the duchess had mentioned the absence of his gifts and he didn't want to go into detail about why he was no longer sending them, *or* and this is what brought on her smile, he really did like her, as he professed that night on the Newtons's terrace and wanted to be her friend. Well, whatever his motive, it was easier to accept the flowers than to explain to Aunt Minnie why they no longer came, so she decided to accept them in the spirit given.

Going over to her escritoire, she penned a brief note in reply, saying how thoughtful he was to go to so much trouble for his groom, and if he considered it was best to send flowers so that Liam and Flossie could see each other, she would accept them. She made no mention of his compliment nor of his criticism of Troy. After sprinkling sand on the ink, she applied a wafer over the folded notepaper. When Flossie returned, she gave her the note to give to Liam and instructed her to put the rose in a vase of water.

Finally, alone in her bedroom she looked at the rose, its petals like dark red velvet. Suddenly, she laughed. There was no reason to do so and she couldn't explain it. She just felt like laughing, so she did.

Chapter Nine

The weather was beginning to turn warm, the Season was slowly but surely drawing to a close. Lady Minerva kept her thoughts to herself as long as she could, but the day came when she could no longer restrain her questions to her niece.

"Carol, my love, it's almost time for you to leave London to return to Worster Hall and you're no nearer a husband than you were last year. Further, in fact, if you count that dreadful young man who raised your hopes then played you false. You don't even have that prospect this Season." She held up her hand in protest. "No, no, dear girl, don't give me that angry scowl as if to say it's none of my business. It is, you know. I've told you before and I'll say it again, you're like a daughter to me, and like your father I want what's best for you. And I think a good husband is what you need. Now, let's discuss this in detail."

In spite of Carol's protests, her embarrassment at her aunt's bringing up what she considered a delicate and private subject, Lady Minerva ploughed ahead forcefully. She pointed out that quite a number of eligible men were always eager to fill her dance card or to escort her to supper, to the theatre, to rides in the Row, to private parties of various kind, but except for letting them dance with her, she'd turned them all down in favor of letting Edward or Troy be her escort. Now, it was all well and good, Aunt Minnie went on to say, to go places with her brother or cousin, but there was no future in it. Was Carol aware that by refusing offers from men other than her relatives she was cutting off her chances for a suitable match?

At Carol's mute nod, her eyes glued to the floor, her aunt continued with her lecture. Why, then, did she do so? Didn't she want a husband, a family, a house of her own to manage? When Carol continued to keep her head down, her shoulders hunched as if to ward off actual blows, her aunt's tone softened somewhat, and going over to her niece, lifted her face upward, gazed down into those topaz eyes, now so pain-glazed.

"Carol, please don't act as if I'm berating you. I'm not, really, it's just that I feel you ought to be made aware of how you're hurting your future." Lady Minerva brushed back a wisp of Carol's chestnut hair that curled about her forehead. "You're a beautiful girl, Carol, both inside and out, and it just won't do for you to waste your life by remaining single. You have too much love to give to let yourself become a dried-up spinster."

"Oh, Aunt Minnie," Carol said, finally, "I'm not beautiful, not in comparison with Lolly or some of the other girls. I guess I could be called 'passable,' but that's about all." She gave a weak smile. "And I'm not an old maid yet. I shall marry someday, I suppose."

"True, you're still young, but need I point out this *is* your second Season. You might be allowed a third before becoming an object of gossip, but I don't think you want that. Is there not one single male for whom you feel a quickening of the heart?"

Suddenly, there flashed through Carol's mind an image of Overton as he looked that night on the Newtons's terrace. She was surprised, and lest that unbidden thought show in her eyes quickly looked away from her aunt to study the floor again. At the same time, she silently shook her head in a negative manner.

Undaunted, Lady Minerva pressed on. "I thought maybe you'd favor that handsome young buck named Edward Case. He seemed to favor you a great deal. Or that nice Mr. Leonard Parsons, even Sir Marcus Reardon, all highly respectable, all extremely eligible, and all attracted to you. Did none of them strike a responsive chord with you?"

Again a negative shake of Carol's head.

"For a while I thought maybe the Duke of Overton was interested in you, but at the last several occasions we've all attended I sensed a cooling in his attitude towards you," Lady Minerva said. Moving away from Carol a step or two, she stared unabashedly at her niece, intent on trying to ascertain whatever thoughts might be crossing Carol's mind at the mention of the duke's name. "Is there any reason he should feel cool towards you, Carol?" Again, she held up a hand to stay Carol's protests at this personal question, went on to say, "I consider it most strange and unusual for a man of his type to send flowers almost daily to a young woman, yet not once request that he be her escort somewhere. He doesn't even accompany his sister and mother on rides in the park whenever you are included, yet always makes it a point to ask you to waltz with him at Almack's or any other place where dancing is observed. Don't you find that a bit odd?"

When the subject became Overton, Carol decided she'd had enough. Rising, she looked at her aunt. "Aunt Minnie, I collect that you have an interest in my future, and ever since Mother died, you've been a loving surrogate. Because of that, I have no wish to act contrary with you, but I really must ask that this discussion cease. I will never consent to marry just to please you or Papa. I will only marry when I fall in love, and so far, I have not stumbled into that blessed state." Drawing herself up to her full height, she continued. "All the men you've mentioned are quite nice, I'll admit, but I'm not in love with any of them, therefore, they won't make suitable husbands." She brushed an imaginary piece of lint from her skirt, gave the back of her coiffure a pat, cleared her throat, then said, "And as for finding the actions of His Grace odd, I agree; however, I've given him *or* his attentions very little thought. As you know, the *on dit* is that he never intends to marry again. I'm sure that is still his intention. As to why he sends me flowers, I have no idea. I do not wish to discuss him any further except to say that regardless of his attentions, I don't consider him a suitable husband, either. Now, if you'll excuse me, I intend taking a bit of a nap before getting ready for the duchess's dinner party tonight. I suggest you do the same. We'll be up rather late, you know." With that, Carol walked away towards the stairs leading up to her bedroom.

Lady Minerva watched her until she disappeared from sight, sighed, and once again thought Carol's indifference to the duke was only a screen to hide her real feelings. But whether those feelings were *for* or *against*, she couldn't tell.

Safely in her bedroom away from her aunt's inquisitive comments, Carol let her mind wander over all that had been said downstairs. It was true, as her aunt had pointed out, that though the three men mentioned, along with others, had invited her places, she'd refused them all. It was also true that by so doing, she was reducing her chances to make a suitable marriage. Aunt Minnie had wanted to know why she did this, but Carol didn't have the heart to tell her the honest truth—they all bored her beyond endurance. Then Aunt Minnie had wanted to know why Overton sent her flowers but never asked to escort her personally. She couldn't tell the truth about that, either. Aunt Minnie wouldn't believe the flowers started as a sop to her ego after he'd insulted her by embracing and kissing her before he even knew who she was, and only continued to arrive to please *his* groom and *her* maid. At least, that was the reason he gave. It was also true that beyond an apparent duty dance or two with her, he paid no further attentions. She didn't quite understand that, but decided he couldn't very well snub her completely without explanations to Lolly and the duchess, which apparently he didn't wish to do, so did only what the accepted code of etiquette required. Would she accept him as an escort if he asked? She honestly didn't know whether she would or not. Did he bore her as the other young men did? She had to admit—he didn't.

She removed her dress, lay across the bed in her chemise and petticoats, closed her eyes in view of the nap she anticipated. But it never materialized. Instead of sleep, her mind was crowded with images of the duke. The way he looked that day on the small bridge, his booted feet apart, his shirt open at the throat, its full sleeves billowing out in the breeze and his jet black eyes laughing down at her. The way he held her as he led her in the waltz, his strong arm supporting her back as they twirled around the floor, his eyes meshed with hers in a steady gaze. Or the angry way his aquiline nose had flared when he told her not to meddle in his life anymore and he'd not invade hers again.

Finally, when she could abide this restlessness no longer, she got up, called Flossie to prepare her bath, and began going through her dresses trying to decide which one to wear tonight. She was looking forward to the dinner party in one way. In another, she wasn't. The duchess and Lady Laura were giving a small party to celebrate the duchess's birthday. Only the close-knit group that had its formation the night of the first Almack Assembly were invited— the two hostesses and the duke, of course, Lady Minerva, Lady Carolyn, Lord Lynsford, Lady Katherine, Lord Ravenhill, and at Laura's insistence, The Hon. Roland Lippinscot. Carol found the company of each person pleasurable with the exception of the duke's. When she was around him, especially in as small a group as this dinner party, she was a tiny bit uncomfortable. And she really didn't know why. One of the reasons, she suspected, for her discomfort was the presence of Roland Lippinscot.

Mr. Lippinscot's charm had, by now, worn a bit thin. In fact, his manner could be labeled as fawning sycophancy. Carol may not have noticed this so forcefully had not the duke been so adamantly against him as a suitor for his sister's hand. But after the Newtons's masquerade party, Carol began noticing Mr. Lippinscot in detail, and it wasn't long before she realized the duke was right about him. Young Roland was *too* charming, *too* agreeable, *too* complimentary, especially to Lady Laura. Did Lolly notice this or was she completely captivated by his attentitons? Carol couldn't tell, and propriety forbade her to make inquiry. However, Carol was almost certain the duchess was aware of it. Of late she had caught the duchess eyeing his acting the toadeater with raised brows. She was also almost certain the duchess and the duke had discussed Lippinscot and Lolly's decided favoritism toward him above some of the other young swains who gathered around her. On one or two occasions Carol had intercepted questioning glances between mother and son over some flattering remark Roland had uttered. No doubt, both the duke and his mother would not permit a marriage between Lolly and this young man, but to show their displeasure too soon in all probability would cause Lolly to become quite obstinate in her defense of him. Carol was sure they were just biding their time, waiting for Lolly to see him for what he was on her own. Knowing all this and the fact that she had contributed to the situation by seeing he was given a voucher to Almack's and through that, entry to every respectable home in London, plus the duke's anger towards her for this action, made her feel uncomfortable in his presence. But that wasn't the only reason. There was something else, some indefinable thing she couldn't quite pin down. Whenever she waltzed with His Grace and his ebony eyes gazed deep into hers, there was a certain quickening of her heartbeat, a rapidity of her pulse that was almost overbearing. At first, when she noticed these unaccustomed symptoms, she attributed them to her humiliation by his ungentlemanly treatment of her that day in the country, then she decided it was anger that made her react that way. But now, she reasoned, those two qualities should have dissipated and indifference replaced them. It hadn't, and she was perplexed.

Another reason she felt uncomfortable was the way the duke treated her. The floral deliveries came two or three times a week, yet he never singled her out except to ask her to dance with him once, sometimes twice, at each social function. He was always the epitome of good breeding and manners, yet from time to time she would get the feeling she was being watched—and when she looked up, would find his dark eyes fastened on her intently, an inscrutable expression in their inky depths.

When Flossie brought in the tub for her bath and the hot water, Carol's reverie was interrupted. She gave herself over completely to the soothing bath which was lavishly sprinkled with lavender water to give her skin a sweet scent. She rested her head against the back of the tub and decided not to worry about her mixed up feelings anymore. The Season would soon be over and she could go home, back to Lily and Oliver and her beloved Imp and Sugar, her very own mare that was such a delight to ride. She supposed London was all right for those who liked city life, but for her, she preferred the country with its fresh air, its lush meadows and fields which by now would be golden with grain. As she closed her eyes, luxuriating in the warm watery embrace of her bath, Lady Carolyn never dreamed her life was to take an unexpected turn towards a future for which she was unprepared. The first step toward that life was to take place tonight at the dinner party.

Chapter Ten

Lady Carolyn wasn't surprised at the lavish dinner the duchess ordered prepared because Her Grace never did anything in a simple manner, not even for a small party of only ten covers. From the *Soupe à la reine,* the *Filets de Turbot* with a piquant sauce, baked ham with glazed carrots and broiled mushrooms, *Pigeons en gelée* spinach with croutons on through the *Crême bavaroise,* sponge cake and tray of assorted ripe fruit everything was delicious and meticulously served. Not only was everything delicious to the taste buds, but pleasing to the eye as well. Snowy white linen covered the large oval table upon which sat a brace of seven-branched candelabra, the flames highlighting sparkling crystal and gleaming silver.

Carol wasn't even surprised at the addition of another guest, Mr. Beau Brummell. Without him there would have been an uneven number, and no hostess, duchess or not, likes an arrangement of that sort. Besides, Mr. Brummell's witty conversation always added gaiety to any gathering.

What did surprise her was the seating arrangement. The duke sat at his rightful place as host at the head of the table, the duchess at her accustomed place at the foot. At the duke's left sat Lolly, next to her was Lord Lynsford, then Lady Katherine, and between her and the duchess was Lord Ravenhill. On the duke's right the place was set for Lady Carolyn, next to her Mr. Brummell, then Lady Minerva, and between her and the duchess sat Mr. Lippinscot. Carol wondered if it was by accident she was given the guest of honor's place or by design. If by design, by whose—the duke's or the duchess's? But she did not have to smother a smile at the arrangement of the others. Lolly was placed where her brother could keep an eye on her and hear every word she said. Lord Ravenhill and The Hon. Mr. Lippinscot was as far away from her as was possible. He was taking no chances on either man having a private word with her. As the *Crème bavarois* was served, oh's and ah's took the place of conversation, and in the tiny bit of silence that followed as silver spoons began to dip into the tasty dessert, Carol had the weird feeling she was being watched. Looking up, she met the warm gaze of the duchess. Why, she wondered? Had she made a faux pas? She couldn't think of any. Then it dawned on her the duchess might be thinking of her as a future daughter-in-law. In the past few weeks, the duchess had made several statements that possibly could be construed in that direction, now that she thought of it. But, on the other hand, the idea seemed so farfetched she wondered why on earth it had popped into her mind. Well, one thing was certain, neither she nor the duke entertained any such thoughts. Smiling a weak embarrassed little smile at the duchess, she went back to eating her dessert. She had just finished and was dabbing her mouth daintily with a lace-trimmed serviette when Lady Katherine spoke.

"I must say, Your Grace, your dining room is most attractive. I don't remember ever seeing a room more beautifully and tastefully furnished." She was smiling at the duke, but at her last word, her eyes quickly took in the brocade drapes, the high back wooden chairs, the sideboard with its highly polished finish.

The duke returned her smile. "Thank you, Lady Katherine, but I don't deserve any praise. My mother is the decorator in the family. This town house, Overton Castle, and my other estates have all come under the careful eyes of the duchess. But I'm sure she appreciates your admiration. Don't you, ma'am?"

"Yes, I do, Lady Katherine, and since I notice the gentlemen are finished eating and no doubt are eager for their brandy and cigars, let me suggest I take you and the other ladies on a tour of the house. Would you like that?" She directed her question to Lady Katherine, but her eyes took in all the women at the table.

All agreed they would love to take the tour, so leaving the gentlemen sitting at the table, the duchess led the ladies out of the room and to the upper floors, explaining in detail the ups and downs of securing just the right things for all the rooms. The men would have been bored to tears, but the women enjoyed every minute, a peculiar feminine trait that no doubt started when the first cave dweller showed off her well-swept cave to her neighbor. And ladies have always been curious about each other's houses ever since. They were chatting merrily as they made their way back down the corridor that led to the open dining room door from which loud masculine voices emitted.

The duchess stopped the feminine procession, her brow furrowed as they all heard Mr. Brummell say, in tones far more waspish than was his usual wont, "I don't care what you say, I say that pompous little Frenchman can't be stopped from conquering all of Europe."

"I disagree," Mr. Lippinscot said, his voice just as loud and argumentative. "Have you forgotten the battle at Fuentes de Onora? It was one of the most dangerous entanglements to date and while it wasn't an overwhelming victory for our lads, it was not defeat, either. And what of Albuera? Even you must acknowledge we won a victory there."

Mr. Brummell's voice boomed out again, acknowledging that what Mr. Lippinscot said was true, but he also contended a victory or two in Spain wasn't winning the war. Not that he wanted Boney to win, God forbid, but he was just being realistic. It was no secret that Napoleon Bonaparte was a military genius and he had the army he needed behind him.

Again Mr. Lippinscot could be heard to demur. "I agree old Boney's smart, but we've got Wellington on land and supremacy at sea. Between them we're going to triumph over that little Corsican. You mark my words."

The duchess whispered to Lady Minerva who just happened to be standing next to her. "They're discussing that dreadful Peninsular War. I hate to break in on them, but I fear if I don't the discussion might turn into more than just an exchange of words."

But before she could make a move, they heard the duke say, "You seem quite well-informed, Lippinscot, almost as much so as if you'd been a part of those battles."

All eyes turned to Lady Laura as they heard Mr. Lippinscot say, "I really wish I had been."

"That doesn't sound as if your ardent suitor is as smitten with you as he pretends, does it?" the duchess whispered to her faintly blushing daughter.

The duchess took a tentative step closer to the dining room just as Lord Ravenhill was heard to say, "Why don't you join up, Roland? I'm sure either Wellington or the Navy would appreciate having such an enthusiastic man under their command." There was a slight sneer in his voice, as if he didn't really believe Lippinscot was serious about his desire to fight for England.

But young Roland surprised them all—the men still sipping brandy around the table and the women listening out in the hall—by his honest answer. "It's no secret, I'm sure, that my Aunt Craddock holds the purse-strings in my family, and though she's quite plump in the pocket, she refuses to buy me a pair of colors or to consent to my leaving. Says I owe it to my mother and sister to remain in this country. And alas, I have not the funds available to me to buy my own colors."

Apparently by their silence, the men were as embarrassed as the listening women that Mr. Lippinscot would air such a private and delicate subject. The duchess turned around to her guests, said in a husky whisper, "Well, that is just the outside of enough! Let's tiptoe back a few steps then start forward as if we'd just arrived in the corridor. I'll insist the men join us in the withdrawing room as we pass by. Don't let on that we heard any of this."

The ladies did as she commanded and the men seemed glad of the chance to bring this discussion to an end by accepting the duchess's invitation to join them.

When they were all assembled in the withdrawing room and the butler brought in a large silver service and began passing cups of hot steaming coffee to each guest, Lady Laura looked over to her brother, said, teasingly, "James, the Season is nearly over and I haven't been to any of the ridottos at Ranelagh or even a gala at Vauxhall Gardens. And I want to go. Will you arrange for me to do so?"

She gave a sidelong glance at Lord Lynsford and another one towards Lord Ravenhill, completely ignoring Mr. Lippinscot. "I'm sure I'd have a proper escort if you'd agree to it."

The Duke took a sip of coffee, looked over to his sister, smiled. "My dear, you have been told before that I will not permit you to attend any of those public functions no matter in whose company you go." He brought the cup again up to his lips, took another sip of the steaming brew, his dark unsmiling eyes glaring at her over the cup's rim. "Furthermore, if I should relent and give my permission, I would be the one to escort you." He held up his free hand as he brought the cup down with the other. "No, there'll be no need to ask what I'm sure is on the tip of your tongue. I'll not take you to either place. Besides, I won't be in town. I'm leaving for Overton Castle tomorrow. I have some tenant business to see to, but most important, I want to be home for Robert's eighth birthday, which as you know, will be about ten days from now."

"I knew you were going for the birthday, James," the duchess said, "but I didn't realize you planned to leave so soon. Did something happen to change your plans?"

"Yes. I received word yesterday that the house of one of my tenants burned, and he was injured in trying to help put out the blaze. I need to see about him and his family, plus some other matters."

"Well, if you must, you must," his mother answered, then rising from her chair and clasping her hands together, said, "I've arranged for us to play Family Whist. I just love that game and hope you all like it, too. The table is already set up in the game room, so let's gather around and we'll see who's the best player." She walked towards the door, turned to smile at the others as they rose from their seats and started to move in her direction.

"Count me out, Mother," said Overton. "I'm not in the mood for cards. It's too lovely a night to be confined indoors. Count out Lady Carolyn, too, as I'd like to show her our rose garden." He smiled at Carol, a winning smile that would melt even a heart of stone. "You'd prefer that to playing a stuffy game in a stuffy room, now, wouldn't you?"

Carol felt a rise of anger as his coal-black eyes impaled hers, arrogantly demanding that she conform to his wish. But her anger didn't quite surface. She *did* prefer a walk in the garden to playing whist, and no doubt, he did, too, and was only grabbing at any excuse available to keep away from the card table. So, with that thought in her head, she returned his smile, saying she would love to see the roses. He offered her his arm just as the others left for the game room.

The warm night was fragrant with the heady scent of the roses. A full moon bathed everything—the flowers, the crushed-shell walkways, two stone statues of Grecian goddesses complete with intricately carved head wreathes and draped gowns—with its silver beams. A small sportive breeze brushed their faces as they walked, blowing wispy tendrils of hair curling about Carol's neck and causing a lock or two of dark hair to fall across the duke's forehead. For the first few minutes, they commented on the weather, the sweet odor of the various roses, then a silence grew between them, each silently searching for something to say. Carol felt his fingers lightly touch her elbow guiding her gently towards a stone bench at the base of a flowering mimosa tree. They sat down, and for a moment neither spoke.

Finally, the duke said, "Lady Carolyn, it's long overdue, I admit, but I want to make a genuine apology for my actions that day at the Blue Goose Inn and for my anger-filled apology—if it can be called that—that I gave you at the Newtons's masquerade. Also, for accusing you of meddling by seeing that young Lippinscot was admitted to Almack's."

Carol started to speak, but he touched her lips with his finger. "No, let me finish before you say anything. About the night on the Newtons's terrace, I was angry, yes, but I shouldn't have taken out my anger on you. You were only trying to help a friend. You had no way of knowing I'd be displeased by your actions, and I'm truly sorry I called you a meddler." He rubbed a hand over his chin thoughtfully. "As for that other incident—well, about all I can say is that I really acted the cad." He faced her, gave a crooked little smile. "You see, Lady Carolyn, sad though it is to admit, I'm not always the paragon of virtue I should be. In the last six and a half years, I've spent more time *out* of England than I've spent *in* England. I've traveled in all the European countries, India, Australia, and made one trip to America. And in all those places the customs are quite different. What's considered proper in one place, is improper in another. And vice versa." His smile widened, he spread his hands, palms up, in a helpless gesture. "What I'm trying to say is, when I came upon you there by the stream leaning against that tree asleep, I forgot my strict English upbringing. At that moment, I was simply a man admiring a lovely lady. When you became so angry, the fire flashing in your golden eyes like sparks, I—I—" He shrugged his broad shoulders. "Something just came over me and I kissed you. I truly regret my boorish manner. I don't regret the kiss—I'm being honest now—for I shall lock it away in my treasure box of memories, but I do regret causing you humiliation and pain. This time I'm asking in all sincerity, will you forgive me and count me among your friends?"

For a moment or two Carol was so stunned by his words she couldn't think what to say. Thinking she was still angry, the duke said, "It seems each time we've had a chance to be alone since the Season started, we've been at swordspoint. You, angry with me because of the way I acted and the teasing I inflicted on you. Me, wary, trying to make you laugh at the whole ordeal, and neither of us being ourselves. I even continued sending the flowers in hopes I'd win your friendship. Is it all to count for naught?"

By the time he finished, Carol had captured her innate sense of humor and could finally see she had blown up the whole episode beyond all proportion. She was sure Edward, had he been in the duke's place that day, would have acted the same. Or Troy, or any one of a number of the young men who'd been so eager to fill her dance card at Almack's. Still, she couldn't let him see she considered a stolen kiss, particularly from a stranger, a light thing to be brushed off like an annoying fly. So, holding her voice steady and showing no hint of the laughter that lurked behind it, she said, "Please, Your Grace, say no more about it. Now that you've explained, I can see your point of view. And I also take part of the blame. It was certainly indecorous of me to— to—well, to be in the state of disarray in which you found me. I accept your apology and I offer you mine." She smiled at him, unaware the moonbeams reflected in her eyes like diamonds. "Now, shall we say no more about it?"

His eyes gazed at her, taking in all the loveliness of which she was so unaware, then nodded his head, saying, "The matter is closed, my lady. I shall never speak of it again."

"I also suggest you stop sending me flowers, at least on such a regular basis, though I'm sure your groom and my maid appreciate your thoughtful gesture. I don't know of many men who send flowers to ladies just to please two servants," Carol said, trying to keep her lips from smiling.

The duke didn't try to hide his mirth. He threw back his head, laughed heartily. "I assumed you'd see through my little ruse; however, Lolly *did* tell me your Flossie and my Liam were making calf's eyes at each other. Is that still the case?"

Carol laughed then, too. "Yes, I'm afraid it is. I trust Liam is a man of honor and is not just trifling with Flossie's affections. You don't think he's that type, do you? I feel a great responsibility for Flossie and I wouldn't like her to be hurt."

"No, I don't think Liam is dishonorable. He's old enough to be looking for a wife to settle down with, and I believe his feelings for young Flossie to be genuine. I'm sure neither of us need worry about them."

A silence fell between them as each was lost in their thoughts. Finally, Carol said, "There is one thing that puzzles me, Your Grace. If you were as anxious to be my friend as you profess, why is it you never asked to escort me to any party or the theatre or any other function?"

Overton raised a questing brow, his lips curved into a lop-sided grin. "Would you have accepted me if I had?"

Carol thought a moment, then said, "Truth to tell, I probably would have refused you."

His grin grew into a laugh. "I thought as much. That's why I didn't ask. I can't take rejection." He reached for one of her hands, held it between the two of his. "In the future, should I acquire the courage to ask, would you accept?"

Slowly, she withdrew her hand, turned away from

116

his commanding gaze. "The Good Book says 'Seek and you shall find, ask and it shall be given to you.' Therefore, I'd have to wait until you found the courage to ask before I'd know what my answer would be, now, wouldn't I?"

She turned back to look at him as she finished her sentence, a half-smile on her face. He looked down at her a moment, then, with a low chuckle, said, "Touché, dear lady, touché."

For a short space of time, neither of them spoke, then Carol said, "You mentioned going to your home for your son's birthday. Tell me about him. I'm sure he's a very nice little boy."

The smile that had been on his craggy face disappeared. In its place, the moonlight showed a stern countenance tinged with sadness. Involuntarily, Carol's tender heart was deeply touched as she realized this man had been hurt far deeper than one ever suspected. And when he spoke, his words corroborated her thoughts.

"Yes," he said, after a moment or two, "Robert is a nice boy, but through no actions of mine. I'm afraid I've failed him as a father. All he feels for me is fear. I—ah—I—well, the truth is I've spent so much time away from him he hardly knows me, and though he answers me politely enough, I can tell he'd just as soon I'd go back to wherever I'd been and leave him in peace."

"Are you sure you're not exaggerating things a bit, Your Grace? Surely, it's timidity rather than fear, for I'm sure you've never given the child any reason to be afraid of you."

The duke looked at her, a half-smile curving his finely-chiseled lips. "You're very kind, Lady Carolyn, to give me the benefit of the doubt, but I fear my diagnosis is correct. There are some unmitigating circumstances of which you may or may not be aware." He lowered his head, stared at the moon-speckled ground, then looking back up at her, said, "I'm sure you've heard the gossip that my former wife died in a—ah—well, a rather bitter incident."

At Carol's mute nod, he continued. "I think somebody, I don't know who—a child, an unthinking maid, maybe some other unfeeling person has hinted to the boy that I was responsible for the death of his mother. So you see, consequently, he's afraid of me." He gave a bitter little laugh. "My only son and heir, the one bright hope in my life, tries to avoid me whenever possible. Ironic, isn't it?"

"Oh, Your Grace! Surely you can correct that. Talk to him, explain that she was thrown from her horse, that you had nothing to do with his mother's death," Carol said, unmindful that she was admitting to all the information imparted by the gossips.

Her admission wasn't lost on Overton. Arching his thick black brows, he said, "You *are* aware of all the gory details of my wife's death, I see. You must also know that she was leaving me to run off with another man. That makes me a double failure, as a husband *and* a father."

Though the moonlight hid it from his view, Carol was well aware of the flush that spread over her face and neck at the embarrassment she felt at having divulged her knowledge of his disastrous marriage. For the moment, she was also speechless, uncertain as to what she could say in the face of his personal bitterness. One thing she realized quite forcefully. When he had said earlier that he couldn't take rejection, he'd said it lightly as if he were teasing, but in reality, she was sure he meant it. The rejection of his wife plus the rejection of his son was enough to make anyone cautious about how he approached another person. When he thought her a local country lass who didn't know him, he thought it a lark to tease her with a kiss. However, when he knew her to be of a family that was almost on a par with his own, there was a reticence about him that kept him from risking her refusal of him as an escort. Not only his wife's rejection of him for another man and her subsequent death, but the knowledge that he'd dragged his family's honored name through the mire of gossip caused him deep pain. Oh, how she'd misjudged him! He wasn't really arrogant as she had supposed. It was merely a sham, a wall against which further darts of life would bounce off rather than penetrate his vulnerability.

Another little thought entered her mind. Did his shyness to risk her refusal of him as an escort mean that he had no special feeling for her? A *tendre* for her, perhaps? No! She made herself discard this thought almost as quickly as it came to mind. Things between them were just as he said. He'd acted rudely at their first meeting and was simply trying to make amends by his latter actions. He just wanted to be her friend. This satisfied her until another thought popped into mind. She remembered the duke smiling so solicitously at Lady Diane Netherton that night at the theatre. Caustically, she thought his fear of refusal didn't keep him from squiring a married lady about while her husband stayed at home.

She was unaware that her thoughts had turned her face into a cold haughty mask. She just knew that for some unaccountable reason she wanted to end this personal conversation. Rising from the bench, she said, "I feel a bit chilled. I think it's time we joined the others."

The duke looked at her a moment, his face as immobile as stone, then with a quizzical little smile, said, "To be sure, my lady, I suddenly feel a chill in the air myself. By all means, let's go back to the party." Guiding her very lightly at the elbow, they silently walked back the crushed-shell pathway into the house.

As they came to the door of the game room, sounds of friendly bickering between Mr. Brummell, Lord·Lynsford, Lord Ravenhill, and Mr. Lippinscot greeted their ears, with muted laughter of the women serving as a background. As they stepped inside, the bantering stopped and all eyes looked up at them just as the duchess rose from the table, saying, "Gentlemen, I adjure that this arguing stop. There is no doubt as to the identity of the best and craftiest player. I am, and I will brook no dissent. Is that clear?" She looked about the table at all their faces, unsmilingly, but in her gray eyes—a shade halfway between her son's black eyes and her daughter's blue ones—laughter lurked unabashed.

From the doorway, Overton gave a hearty laugh. "I fear my mother is using her rank as a clout again. Has she been browbeating you terribly?"

The men groaned mockingly and the ladies twittered as Mr. Brummell said, "James, you wouldn't believe the treatment we have suffered at her hands. Not only has she won nearly every time, but she has positivly gloated over it. I tell you, she is shameless!"

The duke looked at his mother, a stern set to his features, "Is that true, madam? Have you been mistreating our guests?"

The duchess smiled and her whole face glowed with mirth. "Stuff and nonsense! It's just that these people are poor losers, especially when they're up against an expert. And I shall not play with them again." She hesitated briefly, a small laugh bubbling forth from her throat. "At least, not tonight. I shall allow sufficient time to elapse for them to brush up on their playing before we have another game." Turning towards her son, she said, "Anyway, I suggest we go back into the withdrawing room. I want you to hear the marvelous plans we've made while you've been walking in the garden." She beckoned with her hand. "Come, ladies and gentlemen, follow me."

As Overton and Lady Carolyn fell in at the end of the line as the others made their way to the withdrawing room, he said, "I wonder what she means by a marvelous plan? I do hope it's something in which I can concur and not some silliness that Lolly's thought up."

A few minutes later after they were all comfortably seated, the duchess said, "James, Lolly suggested it first, but I agreed it would be deliciously amusing for all of us to go to the Castle with you and celebrate dear Robert's birthday with a weeklong house party. It's time the little darling met more people than just us and his nanny, don't you agree? Besides, it would be a lovely way to end the Season. Now, don't be a spoilsport, say you approve so we can get on with our plans."

The duchess was looking at her son almost coquettishly, willing him to give his consent.

As soon as the duchess mentioned moving the whole group to the Castle for a week, Carol looked at the duke. For a fleeting moment, his thin nostrils flared as if angered, his eyes darkened; then with chameleonic haste, his face took on a bland look and a soft smile curved his lips.

"Why, of course, I approve. I'm just sorry I didn't think of if first." He looked at each face, his eyes lingering just a fraction longer on Carol's than on the rest. "As you say, it would be a fitting end to the Season, and I shall be delighted to have each of you as my guests at Overton Castle."

It was the kind of speech a gracious host would be expected to say, but Carol's sharp eyes observed a small discrepancy—the smile on his lips didn't quite reach his eyes. And when he had looked at Lord Ravenhill and Mr. Lippinscot, she saw the muscle in his jaw tighten imperceptibly. Did they notice? she wondered. If so, neither gave any hint of it. No doubt, if either man hoped to win Lady Laura's affections, they wouldn't be intimidated by the knowledge the duke didn't really want them as his guests, just so long as he included them in his blanket welcome. Where the winning of a marriage partner was concerned, sometimes men's skin became quite thick. Women's too, for that matter, as she was to learn from Aunt Minnie as they made their way home after the party was over.

No sooner had they settled back in Edward's carriage than Lady Minerva began to extol the advantages of being invited to the duke's country seat. Not counting on the prestige this would have with the rest of the *ton*, it would give Carol and His Grace enough time to become better acquainted, and who knows, she went on to say, when he saw the sweetness and depth of her character he might be moved to make an offer for her hand in marriage. And even if that didn't happen, dear Edward might be able to win Lady Laura's hand, thus tying the Duke's family to their own with strong bonds that would carry weight for generations to come.

At the same time Lady Minerva was making plans for either her niece or her nephew, or both, to make attractive conquests, in Lord Ravenhill's carriage Lady Katherine was voicing the same opinions. She, too, was in hopes dear Carol would be able to secure the duke's offer of marriage, but even dearer to her own heart was the hope that her son would win the hand of Lady Laura.

"Now, Mama, don't get your hopes up on that score. I don't stand a prayer of a chance to win that lady's hand. Her brother will see to that. In fact, I'm not sure I'll accept the invitation. I can spend the time better by staying in town."

"Oh, no!" cried Lady Katherine. "If you can't think of yourself, at least think of me. What a feather in my cap to be a house guest of the Duke of Overton and the dowager duchess. Please, Troy, say you'll go." She laid a gloved hand on her son's arm, a hint of tears in her voice. "It's time you were settling down with a wife, my son, and Lady Laura has looks and money and breeding. If you'd try, I feel sure a handsome young man like yourself could win her for a wife."

Lord Ravenhill was silent for a moment. He knew his chances with Overton were nil, but since he couldn't tell his mother the reason for Overton's dislike for him as a suitor, he said nothing. And because he didn't want to hurt her any more than he had already by remaining a bachelor so long and because he had to be so close with his money, he gave in to her wishes about the party. At least, he could afford to give her that small pleasure. "All right, Mama, I'll go to that Castle with you, but don't count on any success as far as my winning the hand of Lady Laura. I can almost assure you that will never happen."

But, like any doting mama, Lady Katherine discounted his warning as just so much folderol. She couldn't see how any young lady of respectable family could resist her charming offspring, nor could she entertain any notion that the Duke of Overton would have any objections to a man of Lord Ravenhill's rank and breeding.

The Honorable Mr. Lippinscot, as he made his way home astride his blooded bay mount, was having conflicting thoughts about going to the Castle, too. On the one hand, he hoped to win Lolly's hand in marriage. She would be the ideal wife, he thought. Besides beauty, she had a most important attribute, a huge legacy. On the other hand, there was her brother, a large stumbling block of which he was quite aware. However, fate had kindly handed him this chance, and he intended to make the most of it.

Mr. Brummell had no ax to grind whatsoever.

He was going to Overton Castle purely for amusement. He knew James Farrell well enough to know he'd never permit his sister to fall into the hands of a fortune-hunter like young Lippinscot, nor would he permit a man with a secret like young Ravenhill to wed the fair Laura. He knew Lord Lynsford was deeply smitten with Laura's charms, but was his affection returned? That he didn't know, but it would be amusing to find out. As far as he was concerned, it had been a rather dull Season and a house party at Overton Castle would be a smashing end to it. His benefactor, the Prince Regent, was slightly out of humor with him at the moment because of a silly disagreement over a chit of a girl the Prince had taken a fancy to over his objections, so he was at liberty to spend the week wherever he chose. And he chose to accept the duke's invitation.

Lady Laura was delighted at the prospect of some lively entertainment rather than going back to the quiet and staid existence of country life after all the excitement of London.

The duchess was pleased at the prospect of the house party for reasons of her own. For the first time in years, her son had given more than a desultory thought to an unmarried lady, and it fired her hopes that more than a friendship could blossom between her son and Lady Carolyn. When Lolly suggested they all go to the Castle to celebrate Robert's birthday, it fell right into her hopes; thus she quickly endorsed the idea. Knowing her son as she did, she knew better than to mention such a thing to him, but if the two of them were thrown together enough—well, who knows? Love has bloomed under less fertile conditions.

Lord Lynsford made no comment other than he was looking forward to being at the Castle. He was sure it would be entertaining. Secretly, he was desperately hoping he could win Lolly's affections because he was head-over-heels in love with her. He wasn't particularly afraid of Troy as a rival because he, too, had noticed the coolness between Lord Ravenhill and the duke. But The Honorable Mr. Lippinscot, now, was a horse of a different color. Lolly flirted with all three outrageously, but with young Roland there was the tiniest bit of difference in her actions. He couldn't tell if it was because she preferred him above himself or Troy, or if it was because she had known him since childhood. The week at the Castle would tell the story. He was looking forward to it with fear and trepidation.

Only Lady Carolyn was serene. She knew the duke didn't really want a house party at this time, but gave in only to save face. She had no expectation that he'd make an offer for her hand as did her aunt, nor did she expect to accept should such a miracle occur. She did hope Edward could win favor with Lolly because it would be so nice to have her for a sister-in-law. Mainly, she was happy to go back to the country rather than having to stay in London until the end of the Season, especially now that the weather was turning so warm. Then, too, since she'd never been to a week-long house party, she looked forward to the experience. Though unaware of Mr. Brummell's thoughts, nevertheless, she, too, thought it'd be a smashing end to the Season.

Chapter Eleven

The next several days bustled with activity. Liam was kept busy delivering notes to the invited guests telling of the plans for the house party. The duke left as planned to see about his injured tenant and to see that all was in order to receive the guests. It was decided that each family would take its own coach followed by a light carriage with the baggage and each lady's maid and gentleman's valet. Carol received an extra note from the duchess suggesting she send to Worster Hall for her little Yorkshire terrier, Imp, and bring him to the Castle to get acquainted with Guinny, the Duchess' little pet. Tim was already dispatched on this errand with instruction to bring the little dog directly to Overton Castle.

Flossie was as happy as a lark as she sponged and pressed and packed Carol's clothes, matching slippers and bonnets and gloves and parasols to each ensemble. She was glad to have the opportunity to visit in a real old castle, but mostly she was glad to be where she could see Liam every day. Their friendship had progressed to the point where each was thinking of marriage, though neither had, thus far, mentioned it to the other. But young Flossie, with a female intuition that was as old as Eve, could read his proposal in every tender glance Liam gave her. She knew it wouldn't be much longer before he'd find the courage to put his thoughts into words. Even Tim had given up trying to win her favors. He realized Liam had stolen her heart and had started casting his eyes elsewhere, though so far he hadn't found anyone upon whom to settle his affections.

The day for departure dawned bright and clear, the sky like an inverted blue bowl with scattered lumps of whipped-cream clouds floating aloft. Earlier, a groom had been dispatched to The Blue Goose Inn so that the ostler could have ready a change of horses and the innkeeper sufficient food on hand to prepare nuncheon for the entire party. All four carriages—the coach and four plus the light baggage carriage of Lady Minerva and the same two for Lady Katherine—accompanied by Edward and Troy on horseback as outriders, began the journey with light hearts and gay mood. Even the abigails of each lady and the valets of the men looked forward to the week-long party at Overton Castle. But at sight of the inn with its wooden lower half, its gabled stone upper half and the swinging sign showing a painting of a large Blue Goose, Carol lost some of her lightheartedness. A flush of warmth spread over her face as involuntarily she recalled the duke and the kiss he had stolen from her. Fortunately, no one noticed her blush for she would have been hard put to explain it. Young unmarried ladies of good breeding should never have known such a caress as she experienced in the duke's strong arms, his lips burning into hers. But she had, and she could never forget it.

Finally, just as the sun was sinking into the western horizon, they arrived at Overton Castle. Old castles of long-forgotten years were not exactly an unfamiliar sight to Englishmen, for hardly a county was without its crumbling stone ruins or its ivy-covered fortresses wherein had lived ancient Britons, or its houses that have survived the years intact. Overton Castle was of that last genre. It was a sprawling crenelated stone edifice with parts of its original bailey walls still standing, though ivy-covered now. Its round stone keep with narrow slits at intervals through which ancient bows were aimed to rain down arrows on invaders towered high above the rest of the building. The sun's rays glinted off the high mullioned windows of the square tower, creating multi-colored beams from the stained glass panes. The entire castle, like a great jewel, was set in a vast parkland of verdant grass that swooped downward a long way to a large pond of water. On the smooth pellucid surface glided three graceful white swans and around its edges and upward on the banks a gaggle of geese pecked the ground for their supper.

If all this wasn't enough to take away a visitor's breath, the interior surely was. Even those like Lady Minerva and Lady Katherine who had seen ancient castles before gawked like the others at the great entrance hall that seemed to soar to the sky, shafts of fading sunlight stabbing the clerestory windows on down to the tessellated marble floor.

As the duchess and Lady Laura—they had arrived a day earlier—greeted the two families, it was all Carol could do to take her eyes away from the tapestry-covered walls interspersed with huge gilt-framed oil portraits of somber men and woman— Farrell ancestors, no doubt—and to return the amenities. As soon as the greetings were over, Carol's eyes darted back to the huge curving stairway that soared up one wall, across a balconied landing and down the opposite wall like a giant wooden horseshoe to the suit of armor in a nearby niche, to large polished wood tables holding massive vases of freshly cut flowers. The flowers added a warm homey touch to what was otherwise a cold, drafty and ancient stronghold reminiscent of drawings she'd seen in her schoolbooks of medieval days.

If Lady Carolyn, her Aunt Minnie and Cousin Kate, who were used to wealth in their own right, were enthralled by all the Castle's opulence, young Flossie and the two other maids were almost struck dumb by it all. Carol was so busily engaged in keeping Flossie's mind on the unloading and care of the baggage that she hardly heard what the duchess and Lolly were saying. Before following Flossie and the Overton maid up to the room assigned to her, she did hear Lolly say that Mr. Lippinscot and Mr. Brummell and their valets were riding down in their respective curricles and should arrive before complete darkness fell.

Mr. Brummell and Mr. Lippinscot did arrive on schedule. And by the time dinner was announced all the visiting ladies were well established in their private quarters, their maids in their proper places. As Lady Minerva, Lady Katherine and Lady Carolyn descended the broad curving stairway, flames from myriad candles lighted the great hall, and through an open door to the right, gentle murmurings of conversation floated out. Their satin-slippered feet touched the cool marble floor just as the butler emerged from somewhere in the back carrying a silver tray of crystal glasses. He bowed to them, gestured them toward the door, then trailed after them. As the three of them and the butler entered, all heads turned in their direction. His Grace the Duke, splendiferous in a bottle-green waistcoat, matching trousers of the new style that fastened under the instep and showed his strong lean physique to good advantage, with spills of cream Mechlin at throat and wrists, came forward to greet them. He bowed to Lady Minerva and Lady Katherine, but held out his hand to Lady Carolyn. When his warm hand closed over her cool fingers and began to draw her toward the others, she felt a faint stirring of something a bit alien to her, a feeling akin to the same fluttering of her heart she experienced that day on the little bridge when she first saw him. To her surprise, this fluttery quickening of her heart continued throughout the evening, from the time the butler offered her a small glass of Madeira, through the soup course, the offering of platters of roast beef and venison, the soufflé, the vegetables and on past the *Crème à l'anglaise.*

It would have added to her surprise had she been aware the duke was experiencing the same palpitations each time he looked at her. She, too, looked magnificent in her bronze Italian taffeta, the same ensemble he'd seen her wear to the theatre to see "Othello." As he gazed at her creamy skin rising above the décolletage of her gown, a diamond and emerald necklace adorning her slender neck, his breath caught in his throat. He thought he'd never seen anyone quite so lovely. Then his thoughts remembered when he'd seen her wear that dress before she had been accompanied by Lord Ravenhill. A frown furrowed his brow. He was her cousin; still cousins had formed attachments before. Was something like that in the wind for Lady Carolyn and that scoundrel Ravenhill? he wondered. He wouldn't allow it! By God, he wouldn't, he vowed silently. She was much too good to form an alliance with the likes of him, and if he had to, he'd go to Ravenhill and threaten to expose him if he didn't keep away from Carol as a suitor.

As the duke was thinking these thoughts, a scowl darkened his face, lines furrowed his brow. Carol, spooning a bit of the *Crème à l'anglaise* and bringing it to her mouth, happened to meet his frowning glance and their eyes locked for a fleeting moment. She was a little amazed that he would look at her like that, especially since he was so attentive before dinner. She tried to think of something she either said or did that brought such a change in him. Her amazement would have been far greater had she known the truth of the matter.

After the gentlemen had had their brandy and the duke and Mr. Brummell their cigarillos—the three younger men didn't indulge, they preferred the fashionable habit of taking snuff from their small and exquisitely decorated snuffboxes—the men joined the ladies in the withdrawing room. After a few minutes of small talk concerning their individual journeys to the Castle, the duke surprised them—at least Carol was surprised, if not the others—by turning to Lord Ravenhill, saying, "I didn't see you at Tatt's on Settling Up Day. Could I have missed you or were you there at all? You know how strict the rule is about settling up debts on time."

Carol didn't look at any of the others, her eyes were glued on poor Troy's face as an embarrassed flush spread from the top of his cravat to his hairline. Why was His Grace doing this? It wasn't like him to be so gauche, so overtly rude, especially to a guest. A warmth spread over her own face, but it wasn't embarrassment that caused it. It was anger. Before Troy could answer, she said, with a tart little laugh, "Surely, Your Grace, you're not intimating that my cousin is lax in paying his honest debts, gambling or otherwise. Perhaps he wasn't there because he had already paid up and left."

The duke raised his quizzing glass, looked at her with arched brows, then said laconically, "Perhaps." But secretly he was glad he'd raised her ire because he'd accomplished what he'd set out to do. He'd planted the seed that maybe Lord Ravenhill wasn't as plump in the pocket as he pretended, that he was guilty, at least by inference, of the ungentlemenly sin of not paying his debts on time. Also, that he might be paying court to her because of her large inheritance.

Lord Ravenhill forced a smile on his thin lips as he said, "My dear Cousin, there is no need for you to come to my defense so vehemently. I still stand in the good graces of my peers." He looked over to Overton. "There have been Settling Days when I didn't see you, either, but knowing Your Grace's reputation, I'm sure you were there. I'm sorry you didn't give me the benefit of your doubt."

Overton's well-shaped mouth curved in a small smile. "Apparently I phrased my inquiry badly. Please forgive me. No offense intended."

Lord Ravenhill's smile stayed pasted on his lips. "To be sure, Your Grace. No offense taken."

As the duchess suggested they retire to the music room to hear Lady Laura play for them on the pianoforte, an almost audible sigh of relief was heard by all as the tension that had started to build at the duke's baiting of Lord Ravenhill died down. But the harm was done, as Overton planned. Everybody in that room silently wondered if Lord Ravenhill was indeed in the graces of his peers as he had said.

Breakfast was to be late the next morning to give all the guests time to recover from their jolting journey, but by a little after ten o'clock all, except for the duke who had eaten earlier and was absent, were rested and well fed and eager to meet little Robert. This was to be HIS day, the day to celebrate his entrance into the world.

As the hall clock chimed half-past the hour, Overton walked in holding his small son by the hand. If Carol thought the Duke looked splendid in his dress clothes, she thought he looked even more attractive in the dress of a country squire. He wore a frock-coat, buckskins and top boots that encased his well-formed legs like a second skin. When she could tear her eyes away from the father, she looked with delight on the son. He was small for his age, his facial features were those of his father in miniature except for his soft blue eyes and the dark blond ringlets that curled about his well-shaped head. His clothes were such as any son of a well-to-do family would wear, but it was his face that pulled at the strings of her heart. He was docilely following his father's lead, but fear blazed forth from his eyes like a beacon. Poor little tyke, thought Carol, he's scared to death.

To his credit, however, the boy had the courage to acknowledge each person presented to him and make the appropriate bow to all. After the introductions, Overton said, "Now, Robert, come with me to the front drive. I have a surprise for you." As the two of them started walking from the dining room to the entrance hall heading for the front driveway, the duke called back over his shoulder, "Follow along, everyone, we want you to be in on the surprise, too."

Carol was in the fore of the assembly as they went down the stone steps onto the crushed-shell driveway, so was the first to see Liam round the corner of the castle leading a beautiful little Welsh pony, its body a sleek reddish brown with a flowing mane and tail the color of thick cream. She looked at little Robert, expecting to see delight take the place of fright in his round blue eyes. Not so. His pinched little face turned a deathly pale, the corners of his small mouth turned down and his little chin quivered. The fear in his eyes grew even larger.

Without realizing she was interfering, she rushed up to the duke, laid a hand on his arm. "Please, Your Grace, don't make the boy get on the pony. Can't you see he's frightened almost beyond speech?"

The duke looked at her coolly, removed her hand from his sleeve. "Thank you for your concern, Lady Carolyn, but I believe I'm a better judge of what my son should or should not do. The boy is shy, but he's not a coward."

At his cold rebuff, Carol backed away without saying another word, but her topaz eyes were ablaze with fury at his callousness. He may rank second to a prince in the nobility, but he's a dud as a father, she thought with asperity.

"Well, son, how do you like your surprise? He's all yours to ride whenever you please, but I warn you, I expect you to assume full responsibility for him. You must tell the grooms how to care for him, when to feed him and what. Of course, you'll have to learn all this first, but when you do, then he shall be wholly in your care. Can you think of a good name for him?"

Robert began backing away, trying to pull his hand from his father's, not saying a word, just staring at the pony as if it were the devil incarnate. The duke turned loose of Robert's hand, bent down to pick him up, but the child was off like a shot, running as fast as his little legs could carry him, the duke in hot pursuit. He caught him, and holding him around the middle like a sack of potatoes brought him back to where the pony stood placidly still, its reins in Liam's capable hands.

"Now, son, we'll have none of that. You're a big boy of eight years, not a baby any longer. It's time you learned manly things." Avoiding Robert's flailing arms and kicking legs, the duke looked at his assembled guests, forced a smile though his eyes were as dark as thunderheads, said, "I can see now the boy's spent too much time with females. He acts more like a timid girl-child than a man-child, but I'm going to change all that, beginning right now." With that, he flung little Robert into the saddle, making sure his feet were properly placed in the stirrups. Taking the reins from Liam, the duke began leading the pony himself, telling Robert to relax, to sway with the motion of the pony.

They hadn't gone more than about five steps when Robert gave a small lurch and vomited up his breakfast, the ejected matter spewing over boy and saddle and pony.

"Great God!" Overton shouted, "What an asinine thing to do." Then throwing the reins back to Liam, he turned towards the house calling loudly for a maid to come get the boy and take him indoors.

Again without realizing her place as a guest, Carol stepped forward, held up her hands to the boy. "Here, Robert, come to me. I'll take you to your nanny and we'll have you cleaned up in no time at all."

Something in her voice and the smile on her face was like a buoy to the distressed child. Without a second thought, he fell into her open arms. Cuddling him against her breast, sour odor and all, she started carrying him towards the house, but not before flashing the duke an accusing glance and saying,

"If you hadn't been so stubborn this wouldn't have happened."

As she marched up towards the house, she was unaware that the others followed her retreating back with bulging eyes and gaping mouths, aghast at her railing out at the duke in that manner. All, that is, but the duchess. She had trouble stifling a smile and the urge to clap her hand and yell, "Bravo!"

Chapter Twelve

It was while Robert's nanny was cleaning him and changing his clothes and Carol was changing into a fresh dress—a violet sprigged yellow muslin with short puff sleeves trimmed with lavender ribbon—that Groom Tim arrived with the little Yorkshire terrier, Imp. Giving her hair a final pat and pinching a bit of color in her cheeks, Carol gathered Imp in her arms and headed back to the nursery.

Robert's drawn face brightened perceptibly at sight of the small dog, a ghost of a smile on his lips. Carol, taking full advantage of his interest, said, brightly, "Look, Robbie—you won't mind if I call you that, will you? I want to show you my little pet. His name is Imp. Would you like to touch him?"

Robert looked at her a minute longer in silence, then said, softly, "I've never been called Robbie before. I like it." A full smiled curved his thin lips. "And Imp seems a nice name for such a little dog. May I really touch him?"

"Yes, really!" Carol said, kneeling so as to be on

face level with him and holding out the fluffy ball of long silky fur for him to pet.

After Imp became accustomed to the strange little hand smoothing his head and back, Carol suggested she put Imp down on the floor and let him investigate his surroundings. Looking up into Nanny's worried face, she assured the nurse that Imp was used to being in the house and would not misbehave, as she put it, but would give a warning bark should any emergency arise. Nanny smiled, but Carol could see she was not completely assured and therefore was not at ease. So rather than increase the tension, Carol picked up Imp, took Robert's hand in hers and said, "If it's all right with Nanny, Robbie, let's take Imp outdoors and let him romp with us." With her eyes she questioned the nurse and received a relieved permission, so hand in hand they walked down the steep steps from the third floor to the second floor where they descended the graceful curving stairway down to the entrance hall, then on out to the front expanse of lawn. None of the others were in sight for which Carol was thankful. By now she realized she'd committed the unpardonable sin of being impudent to her host, especially when said host was a premier duke of the realm. She was sure he was angry with her and with just cause. Maybe, if she didn't have to face him for a while, his temper would have cooled a bit and she would be able to think of some kind of apology to make. But at the moment when poor little Robert exhibited his extreme fear, she was so overset with anger she threw caution to the wind. For the present, however, she'd been able to win a modicum of trust from Robert and she intended to expand it as far as she could.

After following the darting little dog hither and yon across the grassy slope, Carol said, "Let's walk down to the pond, Robbie, and let Imp see the swans and the geese. Do you think he'll be afraid of them? or they of him?"

Robbie laughed, a merry tinkling sound, and his blue eyes sparkled with unaccustomed joy. "I don't think Imp would be afraid of anything." Suddenly, the merriment on his face disappeared, a veil of sadness took its place. "He's much braver than I am. I'm afraid of lots of things."

"Tell me about your fears, Robbie. Maybe I can help you overcome them. You know, I have a brother back at my home, and when he was your age he was afraid of the dark. We had to make sure there was always a candle burning in his room every night even while he slept, but I helped him to find the courage to face the dark. Maybe I can help you. Would you mind talking to me about whatever it is you fear? I promise not to tell anyone else anything you tell me."

They walked along in silence for what seemed to Carol a long time. Finally, Robbie, still holding her hand, looked up at her, said, "Mostly, I guess, I'm afraid of my father. I'm afraid he'll kill me like he did my mother 'cause he don't like me any better than he did her."

"Oh, Robbie, Robbie! I'm sure you're mistaken. Your father would never do such a thing. He loves you."

"That's what Grandmother and Aunt Lolly say, but I don't believe them. If he loved me, he'd live

140

here instead of just coming here at Christmas time and on my birthday, then going away again."

By then they had reached the pond. Almost hidden under the boughs of a drooping willow tree there was a stone bench. Carol led the boy there and suggested they sit down and talk some more.

Just as they settled themselves on the cool stone seat, some of the geese that were closest to them began to honk agitatedly and a few of them flew away to the other side of the pond.

"It looks as if we disturbed some of the geese, Robbie, but I'm sure they'll be back when they see we mean them no harm. Now, let's get back to your fear of your father. Tell me, why do you think he doesn't like you and why do you think he didn't like your mother?"

A little chill snaked down her back as she remembered the duke's telling her he suspicioned someone had poisoned the boy's mind against him. It appears he was right, but who would do such a thing? If she could find out the cause of his mistrust of his father, maybe the duke would overlook her rudeness to him that morning.

Robbie looked at her a long time before answering. "You really won't tell on me if I tell you?"

"I promise nothing will happen to you because of what you say to me," Carol said, careful not to make a promise she might not be able to keep, at the same time giving the boy the assurance he needed.

"Louis told me my mother was riding a horse and my father made it stumble and she fell off and died. He said my father didn't want her to be his wife any longer."

Carol forced herself to be calm and not show her deep concern at this misinformation. "And who is Louis, Robbie? Was he a witness to the accident?"

"Oh, no, ma'am, he wasn't there. He's just a boy like me only he's ten years old. He's the blacksmith's son and he's smart. He knows a lot of things."

Carol shuddered slightly wondering what other "smart knowledge" the smith's son had imparted to the young boy, but keeping her questions at a minimum, said, "Well, Robbie, it seems to me that Louis has only heard from other people guesses about your mother's death and that he's been badly misinformed." She touched his small face with her fingers, turned him so that she could look directly into his soft blue eyes. "Do you trust me, Robbie? I know we've only become friends today, but that's long enough for me to like and trust you, and I hope it's enough time for you to consider me a friend. Do you?"

"Yes, ma'am, Lady Carolyn, I—I d-do like you and I t-trust you, too."

"Then listen to me and believe what I tell you. Your father didn't kill your mother no matter what anybody says. It was an accident. True, she was riding a horse and the horse stumbled throwing her off, but your father wasn't to blame for that. It—it just happened."

Robbie was silent a long time. Finally, he said, "Then he wasn't really trying to get rid of her? He liked her?"

Oh, how can I explain something like this to a child? Carol wondered. Furthermore, how much do I know about the situation that I can tell to the child without straying from the truth? But, she decided, she had to try. She hadn't dreamed she would ever have been put into this position. She only wanted to help him overcome some of his fear of his father, not get involved in such grown-up situations as love between a man and his wife and another man. She'd just have to answer him the best she could.

"Robbie, I don't know the answer to that. But I'm sure your father loved your mother. He married her, didn't he? And all husbands love their wives, don't they?"

At least, she thought, that's the ideal assumption, especially to an innocent child. She was rewarded by the gleam that began to brighten his eyes. "Yes, I hadn't thought of that. I guess he did love her." The gleam died almost as suddenly as it blossomed. "But he doesn't love me. He leaves me here with Grandmother and Aunt Lolly and Nanny."

"That's not true, either, Robbie. For a long time after your mother died he was so unhappy and you reminded him so much of your mother that he just had to stay away until his grief lessened," Carol said, softly, wishing she'd never gotten this deep into the boy's fears.

He looked at her thoughtfully, then his eyes began to shine again. "Do you really think that's what happened? Grandmother told me once that I looked a lot like my mother." Suddenly, he smiled, the same smile, only in miniature, that at times lighted up the face of his father, the kind of smile that could win the stoniest heart. "Yes," he said, breathlessly, "I'm sure that's the reason. And now he doesn't mind how I look. That's why he gave me the pony!" Just as quickly as it rose his spirit sank once more. "But I'm afraid to ride it. Now he'll think I'm a coward and won't like me anymore."

Happy to be able to change the subject to a much firmer one, Carol said, "I'll teach you how to ride and to not be afraid of your pony. Would you like that?"

"Oh, yes! Very much."

"All right, beginning tomorrow morning, I'll give you your first lesson. I'm sure your father has other plans for today, since this is your birthday, but in the morning I'm sure we'll both be free. I shall ask him for permission to teach you."

At that moment, Imp began to bark at something close to the large drooping willow tree under which they were sitting. He'd back up a space or two, bark, then step forward again and bark, then repeat the same procedure.

"Imp! Whatever are you barking for?" Carol asked, then smiled at Robert. "I guess there must be a bug on the ground. Imp doesn't like bugs and things that crawl under leaves and rocks and such." She rose from the bench, bent to pick up the little dog, then froze in her tracks. Sticking out from under the thick hanging branches were the toes of a pair of black boots. Lifting her eyes, Carol stared directly into the dark opaque eyes of the duke. Quickly, he put a finger to his lips in the age-old gesture of silence.

Turning around with Imp in her arms, she said, "Robbie, will you take Imp back to the house? He's had enough running and playing for a while. Take him to Flossie, she'll make him comfortable."

As she transferred the dog to Robert's outstretched arms, she continued. "As you go along, think of several names for your pony. Meanwhile, I want to sit here a bit longer. I'll try to think of some names, too. Later on we'll decide on the one we like best. Would you like that?"

A wide grin split his small face. "Yes, ma'am, I would like that. And I'll ask Nanny to help, too. She's good at thinking up names."

After he was out of earshot, Carol said, "You can come out now, Your Grace, Robert's gone."

As the duke parted the swinging branches and stepped around to the stone bench, Carol looked up into his eyes, black as obsidian and just as hard. Touching the tip of her pink tongue to her dry lips and swallowing against the dryness in her throat, she said, "I-I-I'm sorry I lost my temper when Robert became sick, it was quite unseemly of me. I beg your pardon. I also ask that you not be angry at my questioning Robert. I didn't intend to get into such deep water with him, but after he told me that he was afraid of you, I—I—well, I just tried to help."

Still unsmiling and still not letting his expression reveal his thoughts, Overton answered, "There is no need for you to apologize, Lady Carolyn. You were quite right. The accident wouldn't have happened if I hadn't been so stubborn and put the boy on the pony. But I need to apologize for eavesdropping."

A slight smile hovered at the corners of his lips. "I'd been sitting on the bench deep in thought when I looked up and saw the two of you approaching. Thinking you were just taking Robert for a walk, I jumped behind the tree to hide until you passed by. Instead, you sat on the bench and I was trapped." The smile widened. "I thought those silly geese would give me away, though, they made such a racket when I dove into the tree branches close to where they were feeding."

Remembering the honking of the geese as she and Robert sat down, she realized the duke had heard almost their entire conversation. "I'm glad you were there and heard all that Robert had to say. Your suspicions were correct, Your Grace. Robert did think you caused his mother's death." She lowered her amber eyes, laced her fingers nervously in her lap. "I-I-trust I answered him suitably and that you approve of what I said."

He stood looking down at her for a moment longer, than sat beside her on the stone bench, his eyes still inscrutable.

"Not only were your answers suitable, dear lady, but truthful. Robert's face *was* a constant reminder of Margaret and her—her love for another man. So much so that I could hardly bear to be around him." He looked off into space a moment, then continued. "But that's all passed, now. As I matured and my grief lessened, I realized I was partly to blame for it all and her father even more so. You see, I thought she was the most beautiful girl in the world and nothing would do but that she become my wife. I made an offer for her without consulting her first, and her father accepted the offer without her consent. She was never in love with me from the start, but I was so conceited, so sure of myself, I thought I could win her love as time went by, but I failed." He lowered his head, made a circle in the dirt with the toe of his boot. "Now that it's all behind me and I can view my marriage dispassionately, I realize that living with a man she didn't love must have been a virtual hell for Margaret. I can even understand how she could leave her baby, her family, friends, everything, to be with the one she loved."

He continued to stare at the ground and Carol leaned back against the stone bench, her heart pierced with sympathy for this proud man who had been brought so low by love that he had no intention of being burned by the same flame again. It was too bad, too, for in spite of his pride, he needed a wife and his son needed a mother. If, by some strange quirk of fate, she was given the chance to become the mistress of Overton Castle and the stepmother of the sixth Duke of Overton, would she accept? She felt a blush spread over her face at such a daring and involuntary thought. Sliding her eyes sideways to look at the duke's lowered head, she wondered if he entertained any such unlikely thoughts about her.

But at his next words and actions, all such girlish thoughts fled from her mind.

Standing suddenly, the Duke turned to her and said, "Please accept my thanks for your help in trying to persuade my son that his father wasn't a murderer. Now, I intend to have a talk with him myself. Maybe, at least, we can be on sure footing with each other and begin anew a genuine father-son relationship. At any rate, I hope so." He looked down at her, unsmiling, and his jet eyes bored deeply into hers. He opened his mouth, started to speak, then closed it without voicing his thoughts. He turned to walk away, hesitated, said, "There's to be a picnic in the late afternoon at which time Robert's birthday cake will be cut and served. Au revoir till then, Lady Carolyn." With that, he began to walk towards the house, his boot-encased legs making long strides, his broad shoulders thrown back and his back ramrod-straight.

Carol sat on the bench a bit longer. Finally, she sighed. His manners were impeccable, his words polite, but behind those dark inscrutable eyes, she was certain lay disdain because once again she had had the effrontery to meddle in his affairs. She was also certain he regretted revealing facts concerning his marriage, that he was sorry he'd shown his vulnerability, let his defenses down, so to speak. Why was it, she wondered, that every time they had a private conversation, she'd come away with the feeling she'd either said or done something she shouldn't have?

As the duke walked up the sloping grass to his Castle, he, too, had confused thoughts. He was amazed and happy and humble at what Lady Carolyn had accomplished in just a few short hours. She had actually broken through Robert's shell of fear, dug deep into the core of his feelings, and for that he was grateful beyond words. Now, for the first time since Robert had learned to walk and talk, he had hopes they could become friends. What a wonderful gift she'd given him! No, he thought quickly, shaking his head and clenching his hand into fists as he walked, she didn't do it for him. She did it for the boy. From the moment he introduced her to his son and she put out her slender fingers to clasp the boy's hand, he'd seen an instant chemistry take place. There was something about her that appealed to Robert, some quality that struck a response in that lonely little boy's heart. Then when he was forced to stride that pony to the point of becoming sick, her upheld arms were a haven into which he could bury himself. No, he thought again, what she accomplished was not done for him. She couldn't care less for his feelings. She did it all for the boy.

Chapter Thirteen

The rest of the birthday passed without any further incidents. At the late afternoon picnic party where other gifts had been given to Robert and his beautiful cake had been served, Robert hovered as close to his father as a chick to a mother hen. Carol was pleased at that. It meant the duke had carried out his intention of talking with his son, and whatever he said must have been the right thing, because now Robert looked up at his father with love in his eyes instead of fear.

The duchess noticed the change in her grandson, too, and as she and her son the duke made their way up to their respective bedrooms to dress for a late light supper with their guests, she inquired as to the reason for the change. When told of the incident down by the pond, the duchess laughed.

"Hooray for Lady Carolyn." She tapped the duke on the arm. "If you are as smart as I'd like to think you are, you'd do well to capture a prize like her. She'd make a good wife for you and a good mother to Robert. After all, in my opinion, any girl who loves Yorkshire terriers is bound to be a winner." She spoke in jest, but the Duke caught the seriousness behind her words as she intended.

He answered her in the same joking vein. "Now, Madam Mother, none of your match-making. You know I have no intention of acquiring a wife. I'm perfectly satisfied with the way you run my household and manage my child. Besides, you know you'd hate to turn over the reins to a less experienced hand. What would you do with yourself?" The smile on his face didn't quite reach his dark eyes. He was too proud to tell his mother that even if he had romantic thoughts about Lady Carolyn, which he didn't, she still wouldn't have him as a husband on a silver platter.

But he had to laugh in spite of his thoughts at the duchess's next words. "This old hunk of stone is vast enough to support several families, so one young daughter-in-law wouldn't upset the apple cart. I'd see to that. As for what I'd do with my time, I'd finally have enough to devote to cultivating my lovely roses and breeding and raising my darling pedigreed terriers." She stole a sideway look at her handsome son. "And, in time, I hope I'd be asked to help with more grandchildren."

"Oh, Mama," he said, using the now-unfamiliar term he used as a boy, "you're an incurable romantic! Not satisfied with depriving me of my freedom, you want to saddle me with offspring just to satisfy your own whims. 'Tis shocking, that's what it is."

He placed a light kiss on her brow. "You go

along and concentrate on making yourself the shining hostess. Forget about trying to find me a wife."

They parted laughing, but as they went their separate ways, their thoughts centered on one person: Lady Carolyn of Worster Hall. As far as the duchess was concerned, Lord Worster's girl was a prime candidate as a wife for her son. She had looks, breeding, money and charm. Why was the man so blind? she wondered.

The duke's thoughts went back to the day he encountered her by the stream at the inn. He remembered the way she fit into his arms, her warm responsive lips, and his heart skipped a beat. Then he remembered the anger in her golden eyes when he met her at Almack's and all the times thereafter when she'd been so indifferent to his friendly overtures. And today when she'd held his sick and cringing child in her arms, she'd flashed him a look that could have cut glass. No, my dear Mother, he thought, you're barking up the wrong tree to find a wife for me as far as Lady Carolyn is concerned. Then, too, there was his side to be considered. In spite of the intervening years, he still didn't have the courage to take on another wife. His love for Margaret had been too deep and it had taken too long to finally uproot it. The scar of that wound was still too tender. He wasn't even sure he was capable of loving a woman again, to take a chance on making a lifetime commitment, to place his heart in such a vulnerable position again. With his relationship with Robert promising to improve, he decided he'd continue in the same path in which he'd walked over the years. With what time he had to spare for Society and the ladies, he'd continue to play the field, escorting those married matrons like Diane Netherton whose husbands were infirm or whose interests were placed elsewhere. At the moment his prime concern was to see that Lolly was suitably matched. And the sooner the better, he thought. That brought him around to thinking of young Roland Lippinscot. The boy was sure to make an offer for her and he was just as sure he'd turn him down, but what of Lolly? Was she really in love with that callow youth? Or was it simply girlish infatuation? And what about young Lynsford? He seemed smitten with Lolly, but how did she feel about him? His thoughts then turned to Lord Ravenhill, and a dark scowl covered his face. Ravenhill didn't have as much chance as a snowball in hell of marrying Lolly, and in spite of his attentiveness towards her, the duke wasn't sure he was after her. Most likely the scoundrel was trying to worm his way into Lady Carolyn's heart. He'd escorted her all Season, paid her more court than was due an ordinary cousin. Well, he'd not get away with it! Once again he vowed to nip that romance—if there really was one—in the bud before Ravenhill could use Carol's legacy for his unscrupulous use. So it was with these black thoughts plaguing his mind that he dressed and went down to join his guests.

Mr. Brummell kept them amused during most of the supper hour by relating some of the choice tidbits that could be told in mixed company of the Prince Regent's zany antics with the ladies, as well as a few *on dits* of other prominent members of the court. But as they all shared a large silver platter of fresh fruit and cheese, Roland Lippinscot turned all heads towards Lady Laura by complimenting her on her beautiful sapphire earrings, which, according to him, were almost as lovely as her own sparkling blue eyes.

Not to be outdone, Lord Lynsford said that not only did the jewels complement her eyes, but the perfection of her delicate ears was the exact background for such exquisite gems.

The duchess smothered a smile at such blatant flattery, but the duke's heavy brows slanted downward in displeasure. He glanced down the table at Lord Ravenhill as if he expected him to put in his tuppence's worth on the subject. Ravenhill looked back at him, a faint smile on his lips and remained silent. It was Lady Laura who changed the subject.

Smilingly displaying her dimples, her eyes shining her pleasure at the gentlemen's compliments, she said, "Thank you very much, Mr. Lippinscot, Lord Lynsford. These earrings have been in the family a long time and Mama only gave them to me on my last birthday. I'm glad you like them, but speaking of earrings reminds me of something I heard today. Liam told my abigail that a band of gypsies are camping at the south end of the village. They have a dancing bear, a girl that dances to guitar music and a woman who tells fortunes." She looked toward her brother, her smile quite beguiling. "If you have nothing else planned for us, James, I suggest we all go down there to see them tomorrow. I'd love to have my fortune told. Maybe I'd find out who my husband is to be." She laughed, a tinkling little sound, and her eyes swept over both Mr. Lippinscot and Lord Lynsford before they came back to rest on her brother's stern face.

The duke noted that all faces were on him as Lolly's suggestion hung in mid-air. "Well," he hesitated briefly, "I don't hold with that kind of fortune-telling nonsense, but I don't suppose it would hurt to go see the dancing bear or the dancing girl. Both should be interesting." At least the prospect of the outing seemed to dispel some of his anxiety over his sister and her troublesome suitors. "We might as well make a real outing of it," he said, smiling now. "I'll have Cook prepare lunch baskets and after seeing the gypsies and the village, we'll go on out to the old abbey and view the ruins. Is that agreeable with everyone?"

All voiced pleasure at the suggestion and plans were made to assemble as soon after breakfast as possible to begin the day's activities.

True to her promise to little Robert, Carol arose earlier than usual, and with Robert in tow, headed for the stable to begin the riding lessons. By the time they had walked the distance from the house to the stables, a name had been decided on for the new pony. Since the pony's long tail and mane streamed out in the air like wings when he ran, Robert liked Carol's suggestion to call him after the mythological winged horse Pegasus. And to a small boy the idea of shortening the name to Peggy for a male pony didn't seem incongruous at all, and Carol didn't try to change it. So Peggy it was called. Robert was so determined that the pony become accustomed to his name that he called out the name every few minutes as they walked around the grounds, patting his muzzle, stroking his neck and since it was nearer his reach, patting his sleek sides. Carol didn't try to mount Robert on the animal.

She only spent the time letting the two of them get thoroughly acquainted, and when the hour allotted for the lesson was up, she was rewarded for her wisdom. Robert's first timid touches developed into brave pats of affection for his birthday gift. As they made their way back to the house, he talked of how he'd sit in the saddle the following morning and guide Peggy himself all around the yard. Carol smiled at his exuberance, happy his fear of the little animal was almost gone.

Holding Robert's small hand in hers and listening to him chatter away, Carol was completely unaware that a pair of jet black eyes watched their progress from stables to house from one of the upper corridor's windows. As the girl and boy disappeared into the house, the duke turned from the window, gratitude again filling his heart at the miracle wrought by this lovely lady in giving him back a son whom he'd almost lost hope of winning.

At the appointed hour, all the guests were assembled in the great hall. The mid-morning sun shining down through the high clerestory windows dappled the tessellated marble floor with light and dark shadows and the sweet odor of the freshly cut roses standing in tall crystal vases perfumed the air. Everybody felt well-rested and eager for the day's activities. There was only one tiny tense moment.

The duke had planned for the three older ladies to ride in the chaise with Lord Ravenhill, Mr. Brummell, and Mr. Lippinscot as escorts, leaving Lolly and Carol to ride horseback with him and Lord Lynsford.

Lolly protested. "But, James, I've already told Mr. Lippinscot he could ride with me and his mount is already being prepared. You wouldn't want me to go back on my word, would you?" Her lovely mouth pouted prettily and her blue eyes were tinged with tears.

The duke couldn't very well change her plans without making it too obvious he preferred her not to be alone with young Roland, so with lightning speed he said, a tiny bit of sarcasm coating his words, "No, of course, you couldn't go back on your invitation. Mr. Lippinscot will accompany you, but I also think Lord Lynsford should ride with the two of you. After all," he smiled, "it wouldn't be cricket to ask him to escort his own sister. I shall have that pleasure."

Lolly smiled. Lippinscot didn't. Lord Lynsford laughed, said, "While Carol is cracking good company, in this instance I do prefer Lady Laura's." He looked at his sister and they exchanged smiles.

When the chaise was brought around followed by five groom-led horses, saddled and ready for mounting, each person headed for his designated place. Mr. Brummell and Lord Ravenhill handed the older ladies into the carriage while Lolly's groom gave her a leg-up on her horse. As Carol was being helped onto her mount, she happened to intercept a glance between the duke and Lord Ravenhill. Overton looked with cool disdain at Ravenhill as Ravenhill's blue eyes shot fire back at His Grace.

Carol had to smother a smile at how adroitly the duke managed to keep Lord Ravenhill away from Lolly and how he maneuvered Edward to go along so that she wouldn't ride alone with Roland Lippinscot. She supposed he chose to escort her more out of necessity than interest because it wouldn't have been quite correct for the host to ride in the chaise with the older ladies while the younger ladies rode horseback. Besides, it was a well-known fact that Mr. Brummell disliked having his beautifully tailored clothes wrinkled and smelling of leather and horseflesh and sweat. She also knew it rankled Troy to be shunted aside and made to ride with his mother, his cousin, and the duchess.

Why did the duke dislike Lord Ravenhill so much? And it was almost insulting the way he barely concealed this dislike by only a thin film of politeness. Could they have been rivals at one time? Or were they rivals now? Maybe, she thought, they both have more than a passing interest in Lady Diane Netherton. She knew Troy was acquainted with her, and when he had pointed her out at the theatre had made the remark that he thought the Nethertons's marital arrangements were ideal. She determined at the first chance she had she was going to throw caution to the wind and ask Troy what lay between him and the duke. All he could do was refuse to tell her, but on the other hand, since they had always been good friends as well as cousins, he might tell her.

Lady Laura with her two escorts rode on ahead. She laughed and chatted away with each man in turn. The duke and Carol rode side by side for sometime, each lost in seperate thoughts. Carol tried to concentrate on the passing scenery. The morning was fresh, the land slightly rolling, carpeted in smooth green grass scattered with splashes of wild blossoms in white, pink, magenta, and yellow, with trees here and there sending dancing shadows over the ground. It was a lovely sight, but she didn't really see it. She was too conscious of the man riding beside her. What was he thinking? she wondered. Was he still upset with her for interfering with his son as she did yesterday? Or was he remembering that scene by the stream when she so wantonly returned his kiss? She felt a warmth spread over her face at that thought, and fearing he might notice, quickly turned away, pretending interest in a huge oak tree they were passing.

The duke had his own thoughts. He glanced sideways at Lady Carolyn. She looked positively radiant in her dark blue riding habit. Her dark blue hat with the brim turned up one side and the sky-blue ostrich plume curling softly against her shining chestnut hair made a very fetching picture. What was she thinking as she rode along in perfect rhythm with her mount's movement? Was she wishing she were with Lord Ravenhill instead of him? At that moment he saw the blush touch her classic features. He almost smiled, wondering if that flush meant her thoughts had strayed to that day behind the inn. Then his smile died before it really began. What did he care what she was thinking? Or remembering? She was no more to him than any other attractive woman. He had no intention of falling in love again with her or anyone else. He looked off in the distance, shook his head slightly as if to shake away all thoughts of her. He didn't quite succeed. There was something about her that kept drawing his thoughts back to her. Was it her eyes that shone like amber jewels? Or her skin that made him think of a warm luscious peach? Her hair like a mass of molten bronze? He didn't know. He only knew that no woman since Margaret had made him feel so alive as did Lady Carolyn of Worster Hall.

The silence held between them until he was the first to speak. "I saw you and Robert returning from the stables earlier this morning. How did the riding lesson go?"

It was a safe enough subject, and Carol answered in detail, telling how they arrived at a proper name for the pony. They laughed over Robert's insistence on calling the male animal by a feminine nickname. He smiled when she told how Robert petted the little pony and seemed to lose his fear of it and was looking forward to being in the saddle for the next lesson.

By the time this subject was exhausted, the small village of Overton was in sight. The carriage and the horses were suitably stabled and the whole party then proceeded leisurely on foot to various points of interest. The duke took the men to the tobacconist to buy some tobacco for his pipe and a supply of cigarillos. The other men replenished their snuffboxes, then they all walked over to the tavern for a tankard of ale. The duchess led the ladies to the shop that sold material and ribbons and other feminine finery. After they looked over the merchandise and Lolly and Carol bought two or three new ribbons, they were then led by the duchess to a small tearoom where they indulged in a spot of tea and crumpets. A little later they were joined by the men and all began the walk that would take them to the gypsy encampment.

Carol had never seen a gypsy camp this close before. What she had always thought of as bright gaily painted caravans, as observed from her bedroom window at Worster Hall wending their nomadic trek across the countryside, were in reality gaudy and downright shabby. In the center of the painted wagon—houses on wheels actually—was a large orange-colored tent decorated with stars and crescent moons and other astral signs. Under nearly every wagon lay a somnolent mongrel watching the duke's party approach with sleep-heavy eyes. As they stopped in front of the tent and looked around, Carol thought perhaps no one was there, but as silent as snowfall, three black-haired, black-eyed, swarthy-faced men stepped out of the tent opening and solemnly regarded them from under heavily hooded eyes.

The duke stepped forward, smiled, said, "Good day to you, friends. We've come to have our fortunes told and to see your celebrated dancing bear."

Realizing these were potential customers and no threat to them, their dark eyes sparkled and wide white smiles creased their dark-hued faces. One of the men, apparently the tribe's leader, turned to the other two, said something in the Romany tongue, then turned to face the duke, one front tooth a gleaming gold, the others showing very white against his weather-browned face.

"We are honored by your presence. Magna will be here soon to read your palm." He stopped as a light footstep was heard coming through the grass behind him. "Ah," he said, "here she is now. She will take you one at a time. The beautiful ladies first."

Magna, a woman of undiscernible age whose

midnight black hair was lightly salted with white, motioned to Lolly to follow her inside the nearest wagon. Lolly hesitated briefly, then apparently deciding she was in no danger, followed the woman inside. As Lolly disappeared inside the wagon, the man with the gold tooth held out his hand toward the duke. "You pay now," he said, still wearing his smile but with authority in his voice.

After Lolly came out, the man motioned for Carol to follow, but she demurred in favor of the duchess and the other two ladies, saying she'd rather be last. Finally, her turn came and she went inside the tent to sit across a table from the stern-visaged woman in whose ears dangled large golden hoops.

The others had all emerged smiling and merry-eyed at what they had been told. But not Lady Carolyn. Oh, she tried to smile, but there was no genuine mirth behind it. The others didn't notice—they were too busy watching the dancing bear perform his tricks—but the duke noticed. Edging close enough to whisper in her ear, he said, tongue in cheek, "Did she tell you that you would soon have a husband and it frightened you?" He gave her a teasing little laugh.

Quickly, she whipped her eyes around to him, saying,

"I'd have preferred that to what she did say. In fact, she only told me one thing, then said she could tell me no more and for me to go."

The duke's teasing laugh faded. "Oh? Just what did she say?"

"That soon I'd receive word of an accident concerning a tall man. That and nothing more."

"You don't believe any of this hocus-pocus nonsense, do you? Surely you didn't let her words upset you?"

She bit her lower lip thoughtfully. "No, I don't really believe in it, but somehow she made it all seem so real. My father's tall, Edward's tall, Troy's tall," she looked up at him, "and you are tall. I'd hate to think of any of you four would suffer an accident that might prove very serious, even fatal."

"Dear Lady Carolyn, please don't let it disturb you. They have to say something to justify their payment. I beg you, don't give it another thought."

She nodded her head. "I shouldn't let it spoil our outing, so I'll take your advice and try not to give it another thought." She tried to turn all her attention to the pirouetting bruin with a stiff red ruff encircling his brawny neck, but didn't quite succeed. A small part of her mind still dwelled on the gloomy words spoken by the gypsy woman.

As soon as the bear finished his dance, something did command her attention, all of it. From out of the tent stepped a very pretty girl with black wavy hair that curled and tumbled about her slim shoulders like an inky waterfall. She wore a bright purple skirt that swirled provocatively around slim ankles as she walked, a thin pink muslin blouse whose wide round neckline draped softly across her upper arms exposing slim brown shoulders. Her almond-shaped eyes were as black as her hair and sparkled like dew in early morning sunlight. She snapped castanets between slim brown fingers in rhythm to a guitar that was played by a man sitting just to the side of the tent flap. At first, she danced slowly, smiling at the whole party—Lolly, Carol, the three older women, and all the men. Then as the music became more lively, she began to single out the duke and Lord Ravenhill who just happened to be standing together off to one side. She swayed, she dipped, she stamped her feet as she circled the two men, all the time holding their eyes with hers. Her skirt flared out as she whirled showing glimpses of well-shaped legs and her smile was seductive as she kept time to the wild and flamboyant music.

Overton and Lord Ravenhill stood as if mesmerized by this sensuous creature, and when she finished, dropping to their feet in a ground-low bow, they clapped and shouted "Bravo" and showered her with loose coins.

The rest of the party clapped, too, and smiled their appreciation of the girl's dance. But not Lady Carolyn. It rankled her that Troy and Overton should approve of such blatant lasciviousness as displayed by that gypsy girl. Why, it was positively indecent to see the naked hunger in their eyes as the gypsy brazenly flaunted her charms before them. At that moment, Overton casually glanced around and his dark eyes became momentarily impaled on Lady Carolyn's cold stony gaze. An instant later, she forced her eyes to leave his and turned to say some inconsequential thing to Lolly about the dancing bear, leaving the duke to wonder what caused such a fury in her amber eyes.

When the answer hit him, he turned cold all over. She had seen Ravenhill smiling at the gypsy girl and had become jealous, green-eyed jealous! So! There *was* more to her relationship with that scoundrel than mere kinship. How could she throw herself away on him when she could have the pick of the Season?

They left the village and made their way out to the old abbey ruins. Overton told the history of the abbey after which they spread their lunch baskets on the soft green grass surrounding the pile of crumbling stones. When all the cold ham sandwiches, the slices of yellow cheese and golden pears were eaten and washed down with glasses of berry wine, they resumed their places for the return trip back to the Castle.

The duke and Carol, riding side by side as they did on their way to the village, occasionally exchanged polite tidbits, but mostly they were silent, lost in their respective thoughts. Carol wondered how the duke could have lowered himself enough to so flagrantly enjoy the gypsy girl's wild dance. The duke was furious that she would care enough about Lord Ravenhill to be jealous of his enjoyment of a gypsy girl. And both were wrong. In seeing the mote of jealousy in Carol's eyes and mistakenly thinking it was for Lord Ravenhill, he didn't recognize the beam of the same green-eyed monster in his own eyes. As for Lady Carolyn, never having experienced the emotion known as jealousy because of a man, she didn't recognize it for what it was. Her outrage was simply due to what she considered ungentlemanly conduct.

Chapter Fourteen

Breakfast was just about over when Mr. Lippinscot told about hearing the latest war news.

"Yes," he repeated, "my valet went into the village early this morning to buy me a new snuffbox—clumsy me, I stepped on mine after dropping it—and he heard the news about the battle of Badojoz. It took place in April, but the word about Wellington liberating the city from the French is just now filtering down to all the smaller towns and villages. In fact, parts of London may still be in the dark, for that matter. I hadn't heard anything before coming down here, and I usually try to keep abreast of all the latest news."

Lord Lynsford, after taking a sip of his hot chocolate, said, "Too bad, Roland, you can't join the forces. I imagine Wellington would appreciate a lad of your enthusiasm."

In addition, Carol thought to herself, you would also like to see him go to the army, leaving you a clear field to pursue Lady Laura. She looked over at her brother, a soft sympathic gleam in her topaz eyes.

At Mr. Lippinscot's next words, she saw that Edward wasn't the only one at the table who wished him out of the way.

"Yes," Roland said, sighing, "I would like to do my part for dear old England, but I have another dream, too. I could be quite content being a country squire with a loving wife at my side and a swarm of healthy children around my hearth." He gave Lolly a swift glance, then smiled. "Indeed, that would be a very satisfactory life, methinks."

Lady Laura blushed modestly as she bent her head to partake of a hot muffin. No one made any comment at all, but Carol saw the thunderous look in the duke's dark eyes, the tightening of his jaws and the angry flare of his nostrils. Poor Roland, she thought, he doesn't stand a chance of having either of his dreams come true.

It was then the duchess announced her plans for their last night together at the Castle. "I think it would be a stunning idea," she said, clasping her hands together, "to end our house party on a grand scale. I thought about a *bal masqué*. How does that suit everybody?" Without waiting for comments, she went on to say, "I'd invite several of our neighbors, bring in some local musicians and have the servants decorate the ballroom with swags of bunting and lots of ferns and flowers from the garden and the greenhouse. What do you think, James?"

"It's rather short notice, isn't it, Mama? Especially if you insist everyone come in costume."

Lady Laura spoke up, her blue eyes afire with delight. "Oh, Mama, that's a splendid idea, and James," she said, turning towards her brother, "Liam and the other grooms could hand deliver the invitations this afternoon, and we'd all have three whole days to fashion a proper costume. There's plenty of old clothes and material stored in trunks up in the garret, so none of us should be hard put to find something suitable." she clapped her hands in glee. "It's such a capital idea, Mama. I'm ever so grateful you thought of it." She caught her lower lip between small white teeth as she thought a minute, then announced, "I think I'll go as Juliet."

"Naturally," the duke said, dryly. "And," he said, looking over to Lord Lynsford, "no doubt you'll go as Romeo, or," he commented as he shifted his glance to Mr. Lippinscot, "perhaps you'd favor that part."

Both young men knew they were being ribbed and Mr. Lippinscot had the grace to blush. Not Lord Lynsford. He grinned unabashedly, saying, "Why, I think that would be excellent casting, Your Grace. I should enjoy playing Romeo to Lady Laura's Juliet."

"I was sure you would," Overton said jejunely. Then suddenly smiling at the group he said, "Since I'm sure the duchess will start immediately on the invitations and will need the assistance of Lady Minerva and Lady Katherine, how about the rest of you joining me in a ride? I need to see one of my tenants, but that will only take a minute or two, then I'd like to show you the kennels and the dairy herd. I'm rather proud of that. The first of these cattle were imported from the island of Jersey and their breeding has been carefully controlled ever since. There's no richer milk to be found anywhere in all England than here at the Castle."

They all agreed they'd like to ride, and as soon

as breakfast was over repaired to their separate rooms to don appropriate apparel.

Before Carol went into her bedroom to change, she visited Robert in the nursery to tell him his riding lesson would have to be postponed until after lunch, to which he happily agreed. Then she went in to let Flossie help her with her riding habit.

As Flossie was re-doing her hair to better accommodate her riding derby—today she chose to wear her green habit with black bowler and shiny black boots—Carol remarked that it was nice to see a man as proud of his land and animals as was the Duke of Overton.

Flossie agreed, then went on to say how well-liked he was by all his people. "Liam says there's no better man in the whole country to work for than the duke. He's a bit hard on 'em at times, but always fair. Generous, too. And he never acts top-lofty with 'em." She said several more things, all prefaced with "Liam says."

Carol smiled. "You and Liam must be fairly well-acquainted by now. Is there anything serious between you two?"

Flossie's pink cheeks turned a darker shade and she giggled, slightly embarrassed. "Truth to tell, ma'am, 'tis a bit serious. He's talked of marriage and making a trip to Worster to see Pa, but we haven't set no date, yet." She gave a final pat to Carol's hair, laid down the hairbrush and with a sad look on her pert little face, said, "I'm sort of in a farradiddle about it all, ma'am."

"You mean you're not sure you're in love with Liam?"

"No. Ma'am, it ain't that. I love him, all right,

it's—it's—well, Liam wouldn't leave Overton Castle and I don't want to quit being your abigail nor live so far from my folks."

"Flossie, dear, if you're grown-up enough to be thinking about marriage, you'll have to be grown-up enough to leave your parents to live with your husband. I'd like for you to continue to be my abigail, too, but I'm sure His Grace and his mother would find a very suitable arrangement for you here. You'd be happy, I'm sure. Besides, it's only a three-hour ride to Worster, you could go and return in one day."

Flossie looked at her mistress a moment in silence, then her eyes gleaming wickedly, she asked, "Is there any chance you'd ever live here, too? If that should happen, I know I'd be happy."

For a second or two a slight scowl furrowed Carol's smooth brow, and thinking she'd offended, Flossie spoke up again, "Oh, ma'am, I didn't mean to be so forward. I shouldn't have said what I did."

"No, it's all right, Flossie. I'm not up in the boughs over it. But, to answer your question, I'm quite sure there's no chance I'll be asked to live at Overton Castle. In the first place, His Grace has no intention of marrying again and if he did, I'm sure he wouldn't pick me. It seems every time we have a private conversation either he says or does something that irritates me, or vice versa." She smiled—a little sadly Flossie thought—then said, "Don't count on anything like that, Flossie. Just make up your mind if Liam is the man you want to marry. If he is, then forget everything else."

As Carol left the room to join the others, Flossie had a few more thoughts of her own. She'd seen the way the duke had looked at her mistress when he thought no one was observing him; also, she'd seen Lady Carolyn cast a few undercover glances at him. She decided she'd talk things over with Liam. He was smart. He'd be able to tell if there was anything between his master and her mistress, and if so, together they might figure a way to bring it out into the open.

By the time the riders returned, nuncheon was prepared. And it was a good thing they returned when they did because an early summer thundershower was brewing. The sun had disappeared behind dark billowing clouds and not a single spot of blue sky was showing. Just as they sat down at the table and the food was being served, big raindrops splashed against the mullioned windows, followed by flashes of lightning and claps of thunder. Then the rain came down in earnest, great sheets of it blowing against the stone walls.

The rain cancelled Robert's riding lesson, but Carol pacified him by promising to go to the library and find a really interesting book to read to him.

The library was her most favorite place in all the Castle. It was a very large room. She estimated almost twenty thousand volumes were housed there. The Italian black grain marble fireplace was topped by a huge tapestry that depicted the crowning of King Arthur. Lifesize wooden statues on each side of the tapestry went almost to the ceiling and the heavily-carved frontispiece did reach the ceiling which was covered by a painting that might have been painted by the illustrious Botticelli himself. To the left of the fireplace was a spiral staircase partially enclosed in the same beautifully polished wood paneling that was used throughout the entire room. There was a lacy brass railing topped by a wooden bannister around the small spiral stairs that led to the gallery, which was also surrounded by a matching brass rail. Servants had already lighted the candles in the room before Lady Carolyn entered, so the rail, as well as the polished paneling, gleamed brightly in the otherwise somber room. But what astonished Carol the most, on ascending to the gallery, was discovering Lady Laura sitting on the floor in the semi-dark passageway behind the chimney.

"Why, Lolly!" cried Carol, almost breathless from surprise, "What on earth are you doing here, of all places? Are you hiding from something or someone?"

Lolly sighed. "In a way I suppose I am. I guess I'm hiding from myself. This has always been my secret place ever since I was a little girl. When I don't want anyone to find me or I have a lot of thinking to do, I come here. Even if someone comes into the library, they hardly ever come up here."

Carol looked at the passageway. It had no shelves, held no books, it was only a convenience to go from one end of the gallery to the other. She could certainly see why it would be a safe place for a person to hide. But what was Lolly hiding from? They had become close enough for Carol to feel free to ask, so she did.

Again Lolly sighed, patted a place beside her for Carol to sit down. After both girls were comfortably situated, Lolly said, "Mama would say I've gotten myself in a Predicament. And I think she'd be right."

"Whatever have you done, Lolly? Surely nothing so serious that you should worry over it."

"I think Edward and Roland are going to James to make an offer for me and I don't know which one I'd take. I think that's serious, don't you?"

Carol's brows lifted. "Yes," she agreed, letting out her breath, "that's serious, all right. But I thought you were sure you were in love with Roland at the beginning of the Season. Have you changed your mind?" She wanted to tell her friend that she didn't stand a chance of her brother letting her accept an offer from Mr. Lippinscot, but thought this wasn't the time for that much truth to come out. She wanted to hear what Lolly had decided about that young man.

"I know," said Lolly, "and I've encouraged him to believe I think more highly of him than I do. That's part of the problem. I've wronged him by letting him fall in love with me while I've been falling out of love with him. Whenever we'd meet after we grew up, he was so charming, then all the time in London he was so attentive and tried to please me in every way, but—" Her voice trailed off, she looked at Carol pleadingly. "But, lately, he's *too* charming, *too* ubiquitous, besides, all he talks about is wanting to go off to join the army. I don't want a husband who thinks more of fighting than he does of me!"

Carol smiled to herself, satisfied that her friend would not be hurt when the duke turned down Roland's offer of marriage. And she didn't waste any sympathy on the young man, either, for she agreed with the duke he was only after Lolly's legacy. But what about Edward? How did Lolly feel about him? She would feel badly if Edward got hurt in this lopsided triangle.

"And Edward? How do you feel about him, Lolly?"

Lolly smiled for the first time. "Oh, Carol, I-I-really think I'm in love with him. He's such a gentleman and says such jolly things. I think marriage to him would be quite amusing." Her smile grew secretive, she lowered her head a bit, said, "And he says such sweet things, too, when we've had a chance to be alone."

Carol hugged her. "Don't worry anymore, Lolly. I have a feeling everything will come out all right. I dare say Mr. Lippinscot may feel a bit sad when the duke refuses his offer, but he'll get over it. And if you really love Edward, I believe your brother will see to it that you get him. Maybe not right away, but in the long run. I—" Her words broke in mid-air as both of them heard someone enter the library. Carol peeped around the passageway and through the brass railing saw the duke followed by Mr. Lippinscot come into the room. Overton sat in one of the Scalamandre-damask upholstered chairs that flanked either side of the fireplace, indicated to Mr. Lippinscot to occupy the other.

"We've got to get out of here, Lolly," Carol whispered, "Neither of us can be caught eavesdropping. The duke would be furious. Besides, I've promised to read to Robert." With that she arose, tried to help Lolly up from her sitting position, but Lolly wouldn't budge.

"No!" Lolly whispered back, "you go, but I'm staying. I don't care if it's eavesdropping or not, I want to hear what takes place. A coach and four couldn't drag me away."

Carol couldn't waste time arguing with Lolly, so purposely dropping one of the books she'd taken from the shelf so her presence would be known, she walked out of the passageway, feigning surprise as she looked at the two men sitting silently in their chairs.

Both men rose as they looked up and saw her, but with a smile, she said, "Please don't let me disturb you, I'm on my way down and on to the nursery. I promised to read to Robert this rainy afternoon. I think it'll keep us both occupied."

Mr. Lippinscot merely smiled, but the duke's dark eyes gleamed with delight and he smiled broadly. "Why, that's most kind of you, Lady Carolyn. I envy my son such pleasure."

Carol's smile widened. "Thank you, Your Grace. Any time you find yourself in a position where you cannot read, I'll be glad to oblige."

As she left the room, she heard his low chuckle her tartness brought forth.

Chapter Fifteen

Carol had been in the nursery with Robert about forty-five minutes. She hadn't had enough time in the library to select an appropriate child's book before encountering Lolly, so she only had the two books she'd taken in haste—a history book and one of mythology. Instead of reading, she used the book facts as a basis and talked to Robert about the history of his country and about the mythical horse after whom his own pony was named. Robert had felt no ill-treatment at not being read to, but was, in fact, much more delighted by Carol's artful manner of story-telling. So engrossed were they that neither heard the low knock on the door until it was repeated. Nanny, who had been lulled to dozing in her chair by Carol's words, jumped awake to answer the door. It was Mr. Brummell.

"Why, sir," said Carol, "what a pleasant surprise. What brings you all the way up to the nursery? Are you interested in story-telling, too?"

He laughed. "From such a charming lady as yourself, I'd gladly listen to a recital of the alphabet, but I'm afraid I have something else in mind. I've come to say goodbye."

"You're leaving, Mr. Brummell? Not even staying for the ball?"

"One of my grooms has just ridden out from London with a summons from the Prince Regent. Some matter has come up that he thinks important enough to discuss with me. I'll be leaving as soon as my valet is finished packing." He came over to stand beside young Robert. Placing a hand on his small head, he said, "But I couldn't leave without saying goodbye to you, Master Robert, and to wish you another year of continued health and happiness. Perhaps I may be fortunate enough to come to your birthday celebration next year, but if not, please know you have my best wishes. You're a fine lad, and some day will grow into a fine man like your father."

Robert smiled. "Thank you, Sir. That is my wish, too."

Turning to Carol, he enclosed her slender hand in both of his. "And to you, Lady Carolyn, I wish you best wishes and happiness, too. I shall look forward to seeing you again in London before the end of the Season."

"Thank you for your good wishes, Mr. Brummell, but I don't plan on returning to London. I'm going back to Worster Hall when I leave here. This year's Season was no more successful for me than last year's, and I shall not return for a third. My father will be disappointed, but I shall be happy living with my younger sister and brother and taking care of my animals. 'Tis better, I think, than marriage just for convenience sake. Don't you agree?"

"I'm not sure, my lady, but I predict you won't stay in the single state too much longer. I have reason to believe you will receive a most handsome offer from a source on which you hadn't counted." He smiled, a mischievous expression on his handsome face. "Don't count yourself out of the marital race too soon."

Before she could slake her curiosity aroused by his strange answer a servant came to tell Mr. Brummell his valet was packed and waiting for him so that they could depart. He lifted her hand to his lips in a gallant kiss of farewell, told her again how much he enjoyed being with her on so many occasions lately, then went down the stairs to join his valet.

As she watched him descending the stairs, the gypsy's warning flashed into her mind. Was Mr. Brummell the man who would be hurt in an accident? He wasn't actually tall, neither could he be considered short. With a measure of distress, she tried to dismiss the gypsy's words as meaningless, silently and fervently wishing him a safe journey back to London. When she looked out of the nursery window, she found, to her relief, the summer storm had spent itself and a low westerly sun was painting the sky in brilliant shades of scarlet and pink and gold. At least, Mr. Brummel would have good weather in his favor for his journey.

She took her leave of Robert, promising to see him again in the morning for another riding lesson, and was nearly at her bedroom door when Lolly came bouncing up the stairs, calling out to her.

"Lolly! What's the matter? Is the devil at your heels?" Carol laughed as she waited for her friend to rush down the hall to her side.

"No," replied Lady Laura, grinning widely, "not

the devil, but Cupid. I think he's aiming one of his arrows at me."

Carol opened the door to her bedroom, gestured for Lolly to enter. "In that case, tell me about it. Did Mr. Lippinscot make an offer, and you accepted after all?"

"Let me get my breath, and I'll tell you everything I heard as I hid in the library. Believe me, it was exciting." She sat down, drew in a few breaths of air as Carol seated herself beside her, then began to tell of her eavesdropping.

Mr. Lippinscot made an offer of marriage, right enough, Lolly told her, but her brother turned him down. However, since Roland and his family were no strangers to the duke, he gently took the sting out of his refusal to the young man by offering to buy him a pair of colors and see him off to join Wellington's army on the Penisula. Even offered to make things right with his starchy aunt and mealy-mouthed mother over his leaving. Roland was overjoyed and left the library as happy as a child with a new toy.

"He was just a fortune-hunter, after all, Carol," concluded Lolly. "And I'm glad to be rid of him, but you know, it hurt a bit to know it wasn't me at all he was interested in, only my legacy." She made a pouting *moue*. "Sometimes being rich can be a drawback."

"I agree. Last Season I had an experience with a fortune-hunter myself, and though I'm glad I escaped his clutches, I have to admit it did hurt a little to realize my money was more attractive than I. That's why I've been so leery this Season, letting Troy or Edward escort me rather than some of the others who asked. I was afraid of a repeat performance." She leaned forward, laid her hand on Lolly's knee. "But what's all this about Cupid flinging an arrow at you?"

"I'm coming to that, dearest Carol," Lolly laughed, her dimples winking from her sweet face. "I think you'll be pleased about it, too.

"It seems as Roland took his leave from the library, Lord Lynsford was just about to knock on the door. The duke invited him in and the two began to converse. That's when Edward made *his* offer of marriage to the duke."

Here Lolly paused in her narration, heightening the drama a bit longer.

"Well?" prodded Carol. "Did he accept Edward's offer or not?"

Lolly smiled. "Neither one. He told Edward he wanted to be sure I knew my own mind before accepting an offer from anyone, but he gave Edward permission to pay his addresses to me so that we both could get better acquainted. Then, after a reasonable length of time, if both of us were of the same mind, he'd give us his blessings. I think James showed good judgment, don't you?"

Carol thought back to the time Overton told how he made an offer for his wife without knowing how she felt about it and what a disastrous blunder that was. He had no intention of something like that happening to his young sister. "Yes," Carol said, without revealing any of these thoughts to Lolly, "I think your brother acted very wisely." She touched Lolly's radiant face lightly with her fingers. "And I hope Edward has the good sense to win your affections wholeheartedly. I should love to have you in our family."

The girls parted to dress for dinner—Lolly eager to have her brother tell her about the two offers and his decisions regarding both, and at the same time wondering how best to compose herself so that he'd never know she'd overheard it all from her hiding-place in the library. She was also eager to see Lord Lynsford, to feel that small flutter of her heart whenever he smiled down at her.

As Flossie dressed her and arranged her heavy chestnut hair in the fashionable manner *à la Tite,* Lady Carolyn felt a stab of sadness. She had talked much about remaining in the unmarried state, but truth to tell, she rather wished love would come her way as it did to heroines in some of the romantic novels she'd read. Without volition, she thought about the warm glow that spread over her that time by the stream when the duke, thinking she was some lightskirt, embraced and kissed her. Was that love? Was that the way Lolly felt about Edward?

She stood up in front of her mirror when Flossie was finished, smoothed down the yellow high-waisted tamboured muslin gown and thought about asking Flossie how being in love affected her. Whenever Liam kissed her—and she felt sure that had occurred on more than one occasion—did she, too, experience that warm glow? But, of course, she didn't. She considered Flossie a friend as well as an abigail and had confided in her more than was ordinary, but probing such a delicate question would be the outside of enough! Giving herself a final appraisal, she left to join the others at the dining table.

Mr. Brummell's absence was regretted, but Mr. Lippinscot's enthusiasm over joining Wellington's forces more than made up for it. He couldn't thank the duke enough for his generosity, until it dawned on him that he should act a bit abashed at losing the Lady Laura's hand in marriage. At his rather clumsy attempts to make up for his gaucherie, Lady Laura laughed, said, "Please, Roland, don't be such a *widgeon!* You weren't really smitten with me nor I with you, we were just children playing at a game. All of us here are happy you're going to get your colors and wish you the best of luck. When do you plan to go to London to see about your commission?"

The duke answered for him. "We plan to leave early in the morning for London, then after our business is concluded, I will go with him to Kirkland Park to help him break the news to his mother and Aunt Craddock." He looked over at the duchess, smiled, "Don't worry, madam, I shall be back in plenty of time for the *bal masqué*."

No one actually mentioned the fact that Lord Lynsford was given permission to pay his addresses to Lady Laura, but the news had been whispered from ear to ear so that all were aware of it and happy for both of them. So much so that when dinner was over and the two of them paired off to sit on the rose velvet-covered settee—Edward frequently smiling and Lolly demurely using her fan to cover her own soft giggles—they were more or less ignored by the others as they played Family Whist. Finally, bored to death, the duke begged leave to be excused, claiming since he intended getting such an early start he needed a good night's rest. He suggested Mr. Lippinscot do the same.

Young Roland wanted to comply with the duke's request, but was so full of his good fortune he declared he could not rest just yet. He promised to go to bed early, even so.

With the duke gone, Carol lost interest in the game—an interest that wasn't too strong at the outset—so she, too, begged to be excused. Her excuse was the early morning riding lesson with Robert. One by one the ladies gave excuses and retired, leaving Lord Lynsford, Lord Ravenhill, and Mr. Lippinscot still sitting in the withdrawing room.

However, this, the fourth day of the house party, didn't end on such a dull note. Not by a long shot.

It was Mr. Lippinscot's suggestion that started it all.

"I say," he began, "what about us riding down to the village for a pint of bitters? I feel like toasting my good fortune at finally getting a chance for my own pair of colors. And you, Lord Lynsford, surely you feel like lifting a glass to your own good fortune at being allowed to address the lovely Lady Laura."

"Yes, indeed!" said Lord Lynsford. "That I do."

Mr. Lippinscot turned to Lord Ravenhill. "And you, sir? Perhaps you have something of your own to celebrate, something having to do with your lovely cousin, Lady Carolyn." He was smiling at Troy as if somehow he expected Ravenhill to agree that he and Lady Carolyn had come to an understanding.

But Lord Ravenhill smiled dryly, a bitter tone to his deep voice. "I don't have a damn thing to celebrate, Roland, but that won't keep me from joining you. A pint of bitters might be just the tonic for what ails me. Let's go to the stables and have the horses saddled immediately."

Arms linked in a camaraderie that never before existed, they made their way to the stables. Lord Lynsford and Lord Ravenhill had their own mounts, having been outriders to the ladies' carriages from London to the Castle. However, since Mr. Lippinscot drove down in his curricle and since his horses weren't used to the saddle, he was forced to borrow one of the duke's horses. The surprised grooms who were awakened to saddle the horses wanted to ask the duke if it was all right to loan one of his mounts, but Mr. Lippinscot persuaded them such a genial host as His Grace would have no objection to a guest such as he, who was most knowledgeable about horses and was considered an excellent rider, borowing a mount. Besides, he explained, the hour *was* late and the duke had already retired. The grooms saw the wisdom in all this and did as they were bid. So, sitting tall in their saddles, the three young men rode off to the village, a silver-ball moon riding in a cloudless sky guiding their way.

Chapter Sixteen

The tapster looked at the three men at the corner table and sighed, his round face full of perplexity. He didn't know the young gentlemen's names, but he knew they were guests up at the Castle and that His Grace would be sorely displeased if he threw them out, as he had some of the locals who overstayed closing time. But damme! He was tired and longed for his bed and there they were calling for more ale. At first, when they'd raised their steins in a toast to the King and Queen, then the Prince Regent, the tapster had smiled. He kept smiling as he heard them toast the young Lady Laura and another young lady named Carolyn. He even thought it fine to salute the bravery and wisdom of Lord Nelson and the Duke of Wellington and their victories, but he began to grow weary when they started drinking to various officers and regiments and then, it seemed, to every blooming manjack in the whole bloody army *and* navy. Sighing again, he turned to the ale barrel and began to refill the steins brought over by his weary waiter—he'd sent the little barmaid to bed about the time they'd started toasting the blooming army. As he filled the first tankard, the idea hit him. Looking around to be sure they didn't see him, quickly he poured half of the ale into the second tankard and filled the third only half-full. Taking the tray with the partially filled tankards over to the table himself, he said, "I beg your pardon, young gentlemen, but this is all I have left. Me ale barrel's empty and there won't be any-more 'til Alfie goes after one in the morning." He grinned then, the smile lines creasing his moon-face all the way up to his bald pate that was ringed with a thin fringe of brown hair. "But if ye come back about midday, there'll be plenty more." He laughed outright at the sad expressions on their faces as they swallowed his lie, hook, line and sinker, and began to rise from their chairs saying they'd best get back to the Castle. As he shut the door, the last thing he heard one of them say was that the duke's horse was a superb mount and no doubt could beat any other in the county.

Lord Ravenhill took exception to that remark. "Mr. Lippinscot, you may think you are a superlative judge of horseflesh, but so am I, and I say that horse can't outride mine."

Lord Lynsford, astraddle his own horse, said, "You're both wrong. I'm as good a judge of horses as either of you, maybe even better, and I hold that my horse, a full-blooded Arabian, is fleeterer ah—uh—that is, fleetester—what I mean to say is, my horse is more fleet than either of yours."

Lord Ravenhill and Mr. Lippinscot focused their eyes, which was no small task, on Lord Lynsford. "In that case, my dear sir," said Mr. Lippinscot, "I think you ought to prove it. What do you think, Lord Ravenhill?"

"I am in solid agreement with you, my dear Mr.

Lippinscot. The first to arrive back at the Castle will prove which horse is the fleetester—uh—damme! Edward, you're making me sound as foxed as you are. I repeat, the first horse to arrive back at the Castle will prove to be the fastest! There, I said it right that time."

Lord Lynsford said, "I shall be happy to race both of you, but I heartily resent your saying I am *foxed*. I can hold my ale as well as the next one and I want you to know I am serfectly pober—" He shook his head. "I mean I'm perfectly sober."

"Let's begin the race," said Lord Ravenhill, maneuvering his horse to face in the direction of the Castle. The other two flanked him on either side.

"All right," Lord Ravenhill said, looking at the three mounts in line. "When I say 'go' the race is on and may the best horse win." He gave the signal, each man urged on his mount and they were off, the cool midnight air grazing their faces and the moon, still brilliant but sliding down the western sky, lighting their way.

By the time Lady Carolyn awoke, donned her peignoir and rushed out into the corridor, the duke and duchess were already there. Lady Minerva and Lady Katherine soon joined them and last came a yawning Lady Laura.

"What is making all that noise?" asked Lady Carolyn. "It sounds as if a band of savages are coming."

The duke, candle in hand and by that time half-way down the stairway, said, "Not savages, Lady Carolyn, but three young men who I suspect are quite inebriated." He pointed towards the large window that faced the sweeping expanse of the lawn. "If you come down here you can see them racing like the Devil Himself is chasing them. The crazy fools!" he muttered under his breath, as all the women, as well as their abigails, joined him in the great entrance hall.

The moonlight plainly showed them riding low over their mounts' flying manes, each one using his hat as a crop and yelling encouragement to their horses like American Indians on the warpath. As they came nearer, a section of the old bailey wall loomed directly in their path. Those in the entrance hall held their breath as each horse leaped gracefully over it without even a single hoof touching the ivy that clung to the ancient bricks.

By that time all the grooms were up and praying that none of the horses or men would come to harm. Slamming the candle he held on a table with others brought in by the servants, the Duke strode angrily out towards the stables. The women looked at one another. Finally, the duchess said, "I don't know what brought on such behavior, but knowing my son's temper, they'd better come up with a very satisfactory answer."

It wasn't long after all the yelling stopped and the horses halted in the back court that Overton came back with the three young men. Evidently, he had not questioned them as to the reason for such a breach of the night's peace, for each man was giggling like a simpleton and each claiming victory in the race. It wasn't until the stern-visaged duke faced them and demanded an explanation for such unseemly conduct that they were jerked back to sobriety.

"Well, it was this way, Your Grace," began Mr. Lippinscot, "I was so happy at securing a pair of colors I felt like celebrating, and my two dear friends here," he gestured towards Lord Lynsford and Lord Ravenhill, "they, also, had reasons to celebrate and decided to join me. We went down to the village pub for a bit of ale."

"A bit of ale? Humph! From your condition I suspect you drank the barrel dry," Overton said, and at the sheepish look on their faces as they exchanged glances raised a quizzical brow. "And I see I was right," he added. Turning to Lord Lynsford, he asked, "Just what were you celebrating?"

"Your permission to pay my addresses to Lady Laura, Your Grace," Edward said softly, looking down at his boots rather than face the duke's angry black eyes or the accusing amber eyes of his sister.

Shifting his glance to Lord Ravenhill, the duke said, "And you, sir, did you have a similar reason for celebrating?" He looked over at Lady Carolyn as he spoke and almost lost his breath. For the first time since this foolishness started, he became aware, really aware, of her presence. She wore a voluminous peignoir of blue voile with a wide creamy lace collar that tied at the throat forming a very effective frame for her fine-boned face. Her hair, loose and tumbling about her slender shoulders gleamed in the candlelight like a burnished copper waterfall. He was dazed by her pulchritude, and without a thought for any others present, looked straight into her gold-dappled eyes.

As the duke questioned the young men, Lady Carolyn had become quite conscious of him. He was dressed in a long velvet be-frogged dressing gown the color of deep claret wine. It was tied tightly around his narrow waist which served to emphasize his broad shoulders and rippling arm muscles. His black hair was sleep-tousled and shone like jet in the candle glow. As she met his piercing eyes, her heart thundered in her chest at the bold fervor that blazed forth from those inky depths. Their exchanged glances lasted only an instant and went unnoticed by all the others with the exception of Lord Ravenhill, the duchess, and young Flossie.

The duchess was delighted her son had finally noticed that Lady Carolyn was a thoroughly ravishing beauty in addition to all her other charms. Maybe now he'd give some thought to her advice about considering Lady Carolyn as a wife.

Young Flossie's hopes stirred. If that look meant what she thought it did, she and Liam could have a bright future after all.

Lord Ravenhill was only amused. He had long suspected his cousin was more interested in the duke than she admitted and that the duke was fighting the same battle with himself. To get a bit of revenge for all the scathing remarks he'd been forced to take from the duke, Ravenhill decided to give him a taste of the green-eyed monster. With a ghost of a smile on his lips, he said, "Truth to tell, Your Grace, I *did* have reason to celebrate. My cousin, the Lady Carolyn, and I do have an understanding that is pleasing to both of us."

Carol gasped, covered her gaping mouth with one slender hand. Overton's broad shoulders jerked into a straighter position, his back became ramrod stiff, and the nostrils of his aquiline nose flared above his mouth, now tightly pressed into a grim thin line as he struggled for control. He kept his eyes glued on Lord Ravenhill as Troy, smiling over at Carol, said, "Oh, do come down out of the boughs, dear Cousin, I've not revealed any important part of our secret. I only said I had reason to celebrate." Turning his face back toward the duke, he said, "I apologize for my part in the disturbance, Your Grace. I'll have my valet pack and be ready to take my leave before sunrise."

Lady Katherine drew in her breath, causing the duke to become aware that all the others were staring at him and Ravenhill. Lady Minerva glanced away from him to look at her niece, a puzzled look in her eyes. The duchess glared at him as if to beg him not to cause a further scene. In deference to her and the other guests, he decided not to make further issues over these silly shenanigans.

Though it was hard to go against his nature, he made himself smile, a smile that didn't quite reach his cold dark eyes. "I accept your apology, Lord Ravenhill, and request that you do not leave the party. Perhaps I was a bit hasty in my reprimands. Had I been in any one of you fellows' shoes, I might have done a bit of celebrating of my own."

Mr. Lippinscot and Lord Lynsford extended their separate apologies. Both were accepted. The duke and Mr. Lippinscot reaffirmed their intention of leaving early for London to purchase the commission for Mr. Lippinscot. Then with servants lighting the way, all of them made their way up the stairs to their separate bedrooms.

Flossie helped her mistress back into bed, then retired to her own bed in the adjoining room. She'd tell Liam about the way the duke looked at her mistress and the look she returned, and see what he thought it meant. Satisfied he'd agree with her that they could hope for the best, she went back to sleep.

But sleep didn't come to Lady Carolyn. Her thoughts whirled about her mind like dervishes, all of them about His Grace James Farrell, Duke of Overton. Getting out of bed, she slipped into the voile peignoir and stood in front of her window looking down at the back garden. The moon was fairly low in the western sky, but still bright enough to see that someone else couldn't sleep and was pacing the garden paths. As the moon's silvery beam fell on an open space between the stone bench and the spouting water fountain, she saw that it was Troy who walked restlessly among the flowers. She decided to join him, demand to know why he told such a stupid lie about their having an understanding. Throwing her wool cloak over her gown and peignoir, she quietly slipped out the door and down the stairs, making her way out to the garden. Naturally, Troy was surprised to see her, but more surprised at the anger with which she vented her pique.

When she finished berating him, he grinned. "Don't be so 'miss-ish,' you ninnyhammer. I did it for your sake."

"My sake indeed, you impudent coxcomb! You just wanted to get back at the duke for all his snide remarks to you. You're as high-handed as a Turk."

He laughed. "My, my, Cousin! Wherever did you learn such unladylike language?"

"Never mind my language, it's your lying tongue that needs to be curbed."

Turning her face towards his with one hand, he said, seriously, "I really did have you in mind, Carol. I think Overton is smitten with you, but isn't quite aware of it yet. I merely prodded him a bit by a small stab of jealousy." He held her chin a little more firmly. "Tell the truth, Carol. Don't you have a *tendre* for him yourself?"

Silently, she shook her head from side to side as he removed his hand from her chin.

"I don't believe you. I've seen him look at you when he thought no one would notice and I've seen you steal glances in his direction, too. I'm serious. I think he's in love with you."

At that, her eyes flew open wide, she drew in her breath. "Well, you're wrong. He vows he'll not marry again. I heard him tell Mr. Brummell that, and he as much said it to me. The most he would offer a woman is a—a—"

"Carte blanche?" he supplied at her hesitation to mention such a thing to him. "Is that what you're trying to say?"

At her mute nod, he continued. "I don't think so. My guess is that you're first oars with him, besides, he wouldn't dare trifle with the affections of Lord Worster's daughter." He looked up at the moon. "No, I don't think that's what he has on his mind. I think he's felt the point of Cupid's arrow."

Carol didn't agree with him, but the thought was too pleasant to spoil by arguing. Instead, she changed the subject.

"While we're talking so confidentially, Troy, will you tell me why the duke doesn't like you. He's made it quite plain he would never consider you as a suitor for Lolly, he's even hinted you're not a suitable escort for me even. What is wrong?"

For a long moment, Troy was silent. Finally, he said, "It's a long sad story. Not one I'm proud of, but one I can't change."

Three years ago he met the beautiful young actress, Jeanne Dubois. He recalled to Carol's mind how she'd seen her play the part of Desdemona the night they went to the theatre. Well, he went on to say, it was love at first sight for both of them, but it was a hopeless love. His mother, as well as the rest of the *ton*, would never accept an actress as the Countess of Ravenhill, and since he was the only male left in the family, he couldn't renounce his title and marry her anyway. It would break his mother's heart. He'd established Mlle. Dubois in a cosy but comfortable house, provided a small staff of servants, a carriage, and a limited income on which she could live. He spent as much time as he could with her and their two-year-old son.

At the mention of his son, Carol broke in. "Your son? Oh, Troy, my dear, how sad for you. How you must suffer. Is love worth all that to you?"

He took one of her hands in his. "Carol, 'tis all the happiness I have, all I ever want. I pretend to Mother that I'm looking for a wife, but I don't think I'll ever marry. I couldn't live with any other woman as—as—a wife. Unless," he gave a bitter little laugh, "I find someone who would marry me for my title, then countenance my adopting my son as my legitimate heir without having to produce one herself. And that's not very likely, is it?" He looked down, then back up, the silvery moonbeams lighting his serious face. "And Carol, I don't want you to get the wrong impression. My Jenny is no lightskirt, no bit of muslin. She's a fine lovely girl whose only mistake was falling in love with the wrong man. She is—was—as—as virtuous as you. I know that for a fact."

"Jenny? Is that her real name?"

Ravenhill grinned sheepishly. "Yes. Jenny Dinsmore. She pretended to be French and took the stage name of Jeanne Dubois. With all those dark wigs she wears, she does look French." He smiled, widely. "Her real hair is as yellow as butter and as soft as a new-born chick." His smile faded. "And she and our son mean everything to me."

Without speaking, Carol gently laid her hand against his cheek, conveying as much sympathy as possible. That explained his lack of money, the tight-fisted way he had to manage his affairs, the reason why sometimes he couldn't pay his debts on time. Remembering the duke's slurring remarks to Troy, Carol felt a resentment rise against him. He, with his hoity-toity arrogance, had no pity for a man like Troy who was caught in a tangled web of love. Though she didn't condone what Troy was doing, she knew how he must suffer by being torn between love and duty, and she resented the duke's haughty attitude.

After a few more moments sitting silently on the stone bench, they parted to go back to their rooms. Neither was aware that a pair of jet black eyes had watched from an upstairs window as they talked in the moonlight, that two strong hands had clenched into fists as Lord Ravenhill took Lady Carolyn's hand in his and her fingers pressed against his moon-dappled face.

Chapter Seventeen

Lady Carolyn slept very little the rest of that night. What sleep she had was not restful. Horrible dreams still clung to her mind even after she awoke. There was her father saying in stentorian tones that she MUST marry, she COULD NOT remain single; then Aunt Minnie telling her that love was not necessarily a prerequisite for marriage, it required breeding, position, money, and respect; Troy's face loomed up shrouded in misty swirls saying he could not live with any other than the woman he loved, she was his whole life; and through it all the duke's face floated about, sometimes scowling angrily at her, at times smiling in his beguiling way that always made her heart skip a beat, then again his dark eyes glared above his haughty nose as he said loud and clear, "I will never take a wife again." Finally, in desperation she arose, dressed and went out to the stable to prepare the frisky pony for the morning's riding lesson. She would just stay there until young Robert was brought down.

In her haste to escape her room with its hazy dreams still floating about like cobwebs, she forgot Mr. Lippinscot and the duke might possibly be at the stables, too, preparing for their early trip to London. But there they were, and there was no retreating after they'd seen her and tipped their hats in greeting.

"Good morning, Lady Carolyn," smiled Mr. Lippinscot. "I say, you're out mighty early this morning, and looking as lovely as ever."

The duke looked at her, observed the dark stains under her eyes, and in grim tones said, "I beg to differ. The Lady Carolyn looks as if the disturbance last night interrupted her sleep, or," he moved closer and spoke *sotto voce,* "or are those smudges under your eyes due to staying out in the garden 'til the wee hours of morning?"

Carol looked up at him, her eyes widening in surprise at his rudeness. Before she could answer, a groom called for Mr. Lippinscot to come over to where his curricle was being readied for the road. It was just as well, thought Carol, she would prefer not to answer back in kind to the duke in front of Mr. Lippinscot. But as soon as he was out of earshot, she said, "What I do with my time is my own affair, Your Grace, and spying on other people is not one of the things I do to occupy my time."

"No?" he said, raising one heavy brow. "I seem to recall how you listened to my conversation with Mr. Brummell from behind a stone column. Was that not spying?"

"Not at all," she expostulated. "I was caught there by error. I didn't deliberately go there to listen to you, while you evidently *chose* to spy on me and Lord Ravenhill as we sat in the garden. *That* is spying!"

The duke's grim expression softened as he gazed
196

at her face, cold now in anger and her golden eyes blazing sparks. A phantom smile hovered around his mouth. "You know, you're passable looking when you're angry, and you seem to be in that condition an inordinate amount of time." The phantom smile became a reality as she drew in her breath at his sarcasm—at least she considered it sarcasm, it didn't dawn on her he was complimenting her in a teasing manner. However, before she could think up a scathing enough reply, he said, still smiling, "You're correct, my lady, I confess to the degradation of spying. I didn't intend to, but when you and your cousin sat down on the garden bench directly under my window, I didn't move away." The smile left his face, he grew very serious. "I have no right to do so, but as a friend I want to give you some advice. For reasons I cannot divulge, I don't think your cousin would be a suitable husband for you. He's not the paragon of honor you seem to think he is, and whatever understanding you might have with him will not signify."

Masking her rage at his forwardness with a deadly smile, Carol said, "You're correct in one thing. You have no right to offer advice concerning my suitors, but since you have, I'll answer. I may marry Lord Ravenhill and I may not, our understanding is not that final, but he *is* a man of honor, you see, for he told me all about his—ah—the love of his life."

He looked surprised. "And it matters not to you?"

"There are more marriages made in England for convenience than for any other reason, and should I enter into a contract of that nature, no, it would not matter to me. At least," her eyes grew colder, her smile almost became a sneer. "He has the *capacity* to love, even though it is unwisely. He's not a coward who avoids temptation by playing cicisbeo to a safely married woman."

At the icy glaze that came over his dark eyes and the cold fury that seemed to freeze on his face, she felt a stab of fear mingled with regret that she spoke so boldly to him. What had made her do it? Why had she allowed him to provoke her into becoming so angry? She had no intention of marrying Troy, so why pretend she was contemplating it? Her mind was awhirl trying to form some sort of apology when he spoke, chasing away all thought of any such endeavor.

"Madam, I have felt the sting of your tongue before, but this time you have gone too far. I thank you for what you did to bring my son and me to a better understanding of each other, but beyond that, I owe you nothing. I will not be called a coward, especially by a chit of a girl who herself is so hen-hearted she thinks every eligible suitor is after her legacy and contemplates a marriage of convenience rather than take a chance on love." He turned toward where Mr. Lippinscot still conversed with the groom, then swung back to look at her. "I hope you find happiness in your cold ivory tower, but I doubt it. Good day and goodbye!"

For the very first time since that day behind The Blue Goose Inn when she met the duke she realized that all the while she had been falling in love with him. All the times she'd felt a stab of jealousy because of him—when she saw him with Lady Diane Netherton at the theatre, when the gypsy girl had danced and he'd showed such appreciation, other times when he'd paid elaborate attention to various debutantes at Almack's—only confirmed the fact that she was besotted to the point of losing her heart completely. Now it was too late! Supposing she had a chance of ever winning his love, she'd lost it now. Tears stung her eyes as she leaned against the stable walls watching with blurred vision the duke on his blood-chestnut stallion riding beside Mr. Lippinscot's curricle as they left the courtyard heading for the London road.

Her tears flowed faster as she saw Nanny bringing young Robert towards her. Robert, whom she already loved like a brother—or a s-son! She'd never see him again, either. At that, the flood of tears broke hot and heavy. She rushed by Nanny and the boy, called out something about being ill, then fled to her room. She never saw Liam, who had been just inside the stable door overhearing every word she and his master had exchanged, shake his head thoughtfully as she made her way into the Castle.

Liam roused himself to comfort the stunned child by promising to personally help him ride his adored pony, but as he lifted the boy up into the small saddle, his mind was on the crying lady and the fiercely angry face of the duke.

On waking and finding her mistress already out of bed and gone from the room, Flossie deduced she had gone to the stable for young Robert's riding lesson. She looked out the window and saw Lady Carolyn conversing with His Grace and smiled to herself. Things just might work out to her and

Liam's advantage, after all, she thought. But when her mistress ran back into the room with tears streaming down her face, that hope took a downward plunge.

"Oh, ma'am! Whatever's the matter?" Flossie said, as she watched her ladyship fling herself down across the bed smothering her tears and sobs against the large goosedown pillow. Running to her, Flossie touched her shaking shoulders. "Ma'am, are you ill? What can I do for you?"

Subduing her feminine outburst with great effort, Lady Carolyn turned a puffed tear-stained face towards her little abigail. "There's nothing anybody can do, Flossie. I've been such a fool. I've r-r-ruined my w-w-whole life by my h-h-hateful tongue." More tears welled up in her amber-gold eyes, but they didn't fall, just blurred her vision and glistened in the morning light. Her chin quivered and the corners of her mouth turned down.

Flossie, though young in age, had inherited a great deal of her mother's common sense and earthy wisdom. Then, too, having matured enough to know love herself was an added advantage. Without a thought for the propriety of the situation, she sat on the bed, gathered her mistress in her arms and began soothing her as one did an upset child.

"There, there, ma'am, I'm sure you haven't ruined your whole life, you could never be hateful enough for that." As she patted and made little crooning sounds, Carol's body stilled and she let her swollen face rest against Flossie's sweet young bosom.

With a bit of cunning, Flossie said, "Mum always said it helped when trouble came if you could talk about it. Now, I know I'm only your abigail, ma'am, but I think you're Top of the Trees, and if you'd like to talk, I'd be proud to listen, and I'd keep whatever you say just between us two. Maybe it'll get you to thinking straight. Was it Lord Lynsford that got you so overset? I know brothers can be a trial sometimes."

Carol sat up then, wiped her eyes dry with the handkerchief Flossie handed her, then sighed. "No, it wasn't Edward. It was the duke. I said some dreadful things to him."

Wisely, Flossie remained mumchance, letting her mistress say whatever her thoughts directed. And it worked. Carol began to tell Flossie about the conversation that took place between her and the duke. As she talked, she paced the floor, the handkerchief she held twisted into a soggy ball. She told about slipping down to the garden to talk to Troy and the duke knowing about it, how she accused him of spying on her and how one word led to another.

"But he made me so angry!" she said, stamping her foot. "Somehow he seemed to think I was going to marry Troy, and he had the effrontery to warn me against him. My own cousin! Why, he began to hint about—" Suddenly she stopped. It wasn't at all the proper thing for her to be treating Flossie more as a friend than a servant, but she didn't mind dispensing with that convention. However, she couldn't carry it too far. She certainly couldn't discuss with Flossie the liaison between Lord Ravenhill and the actress known as Jeanne Dubois. "H-H-He began to hint that Lord Ravenhill wasn't—ah—well, that he wasn't quite honorable," she finished lamely.

After a few minutes passed, Flossie asked, "*Are* you going to marry Lord Ravenhill, ma'am?" She waited with baited breath for Lady Carolyn's answer, all her hopes hanging in mid-air.

Carol walked over to the window. Looking down on the garden bench where she sat and talked to Troy, she thought about Flossie's question. Turning around to face the young servant, she said, "I just might, Flossie. In a few years, I'll come into a large legacy, and I might as well help Lord Ravenhill out of a certain dilemma as share it with some crass fortune-hunter."

Flossie, still clinging to the hope that her mistress might possibly be in love with the Duke of Overton, said, "But, ma'am, have you given no thought at all to the fact that His Grace might make an offer? Liam says he has all the signs of a man truly smitten." She gave a timorous smile, praying she wasn't overstepping her bounds. "And think of all the flowers and little gifties he sent you. They must signify something. And you can't accuse him of being a fortune-hunter, not with him being as plump in the pocket as he is."

Carol answered back with a bitter little laugh. "At first, he hoped to make amends for his rude behavior that day at The Blue Goose Inn, then later he continued to send them because it gave Liam a chance to see you." She raised her hands, palms up, and shrugged her shoulders. "So you see, all those little gifties, as you call them, were really for you and Liam, not me."

Flossie's lips formed an *O* as she silently took in what her mistress said. Surely her ladyship wasn't thick-headed enough to fall for that! No master, not even one as kind and good as the duke, would go to all that trouble for a groom and a lady's maid. Before she could think of a suitable reply, Lady Carolyn said, "Besides, regardless of Liam's prognosis, I don't think the duke was ever enamored of me. However, suppose that theory to be true, it is no longer. After what I said to him he would be hard put to treat me civilly." Fresh tears welled up and spilled down her face. Wiping them away with the back of her hand, she said, her voice trembling, "I'm afraid it'll take a miracle to make matters between us right again, and miracles don't occur very often nowadays."

Flossie took a deep breath, screwed up her courage, and plunged in where even angels fear to tread by asking, "Ma'am, have you fallen in love with His Grace?" She knew by asking such a personal question, she was walking on quicksand, but she was ready to sink into the mire if she got the right answer. If Her Ladyship admitted her true feelings, there was a slim chance she and Liam could make that miracle happen. On the other hand, she could lose her position and be sent home immediately. That didn't worry her too much as Liam would come to rescue her, but she quaked at the thought of losing Lady Carolyn's respect and friendship. But even that was worth it if her mistress could find happiness.

At first, Carol looked at Flossie with a vehement denial on the tip of her tongue, but when she saw the little maid was truly concerned about her feelings and was not being in any way impertinent, she realized Flossie was the only friend she had to whom she could be truly honest. Flossie would never betray her confidence. With a sigh, she said, "I'm afraid so, Flossie. I didn't realize it myself until he turned his back on me. Now I can consider myself fortunate if he ever looks in my direction again."

Flossie's hopes soared once more. Just what she thought, only a lover's quarrel, nothing more, only neither of them were aware of its nature. It would be up to her and Liam to make them see they were both victims of Cupid's darts.

"Now, ma'am," Flossie said, going over to the china wash bowl and wringing out a cloth, "as Mum says, while there's life, there's hope. Here, wipe your face with this wet cloth and just you take off them clothes and hop back into bed. I'll have Cook fix you a nice breakfast tray and bring it up to you. I'll say you feel a nasty cold coming on so you'll have an excuse to stay in bed for as long as you want. Something warm in your stomach and a good rest will make you feel fit as a fiddle again." She took the damp cloth from her mistress after it was used, then began to unfasten the back of her morning dress. After straightening the tumbled bed linen and plumping up the pillows, she led Carol over to the bed, held her peignoir so she could slip into it, saying, "Slip this over your chemise and petticoats until you're finished with breakfast, then take it off and snuggle down between the sheets for a good nap. You'll feel better by dinnertime, I'm sure of it, Ma'am."

Carol laughed. "You're your mother's daughter all right. You sound just like Ada, fussing and clucking around me like a mother hen." But because of the lack of sleep the night before and the case of the dismals that settled over her after her set-to with the duke, Carol welcomed the thought of staying in her room the rest of the day. Willingly, she let Flossie settle her in the bed, propped high against the headboard by two large goosedown pillows.

Before Flossie could return with her breakfast tray, the news that she was "indisposed with a slight cold" spread like wildfire among the Castle's occupants. She was forced to suffer through a visit from each one. First came Aunt Minnie, anxious to see for herself that her niece was not terribly ill, and quite relieved at the promise she would join them for the dinner hour. Next came Cousin Kate bearing solicitations from Lord Ravenhill and Lord Lynsford, then Lolly and the duchess came by to offer any small comfort she might need. It was while she was eating from the breakfast tray that Nanny brought Master Robert to the door, Nanny saying that she would not permit her charge to get any closer for fear he, too, might come down with the same indisposition. Carol agreed with this and waved to Robert, promising to see him the following morning as usual. Only when finally she was left alone with Flossie, like Cerberus keeping watch in the adjoining room, did she discard one pillow and slip down for a much-needed nap.

As soon as Flossie was sure her mistress was asleep, making sure no one saw her leave her post she quietly slipped down the back stairs and out to the stables to find Liam. They talked for quite sometime before Liam spied Lord Ravenhill approaching dressed in top boots and buckskins.

"Floss, what do you say to letting the young Lord there—" he nodded his red-thatched head in Ravenhill's direction, "in on our plans? He's no nod-cock and we might need him."

Flossie looked with a questing eye at the approaching man. "Well, he *is* her cousin and seems to have her best interest at heart. It can't hurt anything, and as you say, we might need his help. Another thing, if we get sent packing, he might prove helpful in securing another place of service for us."

Liam smiled. "For *us*. Has a nice ring to it, it does." He squeezed her hand, looked deep into her soft blue eyes. "Whatever happens, Flossie, my girl, we're going to be together, here or someplace else."

Flossie's heart flipped-flopped as usual whenever Liam sweet-talked her, and her desire to help her mistress know the same kind of happiness she did became even stronger. "Go ahead, Liam, tell Lord Ravenhill our plan, but feel him out a bit first, see if we can truly trust him."

"Aye, I'd already thought about that. You go on back to your mistress now and come back later and I'll tell you what happened."

Flossie passed Lord Ravenhill as he neared the stable, bobbing a curtsy and wishing him a good ride this lovely morning. He smiled his acknowledgement and went on to engage Liam in preparing his horse.

The sun was lowering in the western sky when Carol awoke. Flossie had been right. A good sleep was just the thing she needed. Yawning and stretching like a lazy cat, she threw aside the covers to get out of bed. As she did, she felt a wiggly body struggle to free himself from the spread that engulfed him. Carol laughed. "Why, Imp! Have you been napping, too?" She gathered the ball of fluff that was her pet and held him tight against her. Absentmindedly, she stroked his silky fur. Her thoughts flew back to the duke and the cold fury in his dark eyes as he turned away from her. She was the greatest *widgeon* on earth to have let him provoke her into giving him the rough side of her tongue, especially going so far as to infer he was cowardly and to bring up Lady Diane, at least by inference. Then she decided she'd let Flossie's idea of saying she was coming down with a cold work to her advantage. She'd already told Mr. Brummell she planned to go back to Worster Hall instead of London; now rather than wait until after the ball, she'd go in the morning. If Aunt Minnie wanted to stay for the party two days hence she could. Flossie and a groom were enough chaperones for the journey. If Aunt Minnie decided to accompany her, that would be all right, too. It made no difference with whom she left, the main thing was to be gone before the duke arrived back from London on the morrow. She simply could not face him, not after she'd acted so rag-mannered. Hiding her face in Imp's soft fur, she said, "You were more fortunate than I, Imp darling. You and Guinny became fast friends from the moment you arrived and the duchess put her pet down to meet you. As much as I love you, I think I'll leave you here with Lady Guinevere and young Robert. Between you and Peggy, Robbie won't be quite so lonesome and he'll have something to remember me by." She sighed. She'd tell the duchess and the other guests at dinner tonight that she'd be leaving for home in the morning, right after Robert's riding lesson.

She didn't reckon on Flossie and Liam putting a kink in her well-laid plans.

Chapter Eighteen

Lady Minerva was on the horns of a dilemma. She was a bit miffed at her niece because of the way this second Season had gone. Last year, Lady Carolyn had acted like a Bath-miss who didn't know the time of day. This Season she had conducted herself as befitted her station, but there'd been no offers made. What was worse, in Lady Minerva's opinion, was the likelihood that Nonpareil, His Grace the Duke of Overton, could have been brought around to making an offer if only Lady Carolyn had played her cards right. But she didn't. In fact, she sensed a distinct coolness between them. Now the silly little twit wanted to go home to Worster Hall rather than return to London to complete the Season. That didn't bother her too much, as she had already decided to wash her hands of trying to help her niece. The thought of a THIRD Season was just the outside of enough! What bothered her was the fact that *she* didn't want to leave Overton Castle. She and Cousin Kate had become quite good friends with the duchess and she didn't want to do anything that would put a crimp in that friendship. It was no small thing being on such good terms with as important a family as the Farrells of Overton. Not only that, but she was looking forward to the *bal masqué* to be held two days hence. On the other hand, she felt her brother would feel she should accompany his daughter back to Worster Hall.

Carol solved her aunt's problem for her by insisting that Flossie and Tim were chaperone enough for her, and besides, confined so closely in the chaise, Lady Minerva would no doubt catch her cold. Aunt Minnie protested—feebly, one might add—but in the end gave in to Carol's wishes. And she was very gracious in granting Carol's request that she loan her carriage to her as well as her coachman with the understanding that both would be returned to her the following morning. With all that settled, Lady Minerva spent a good night dreaming of future invitations that might possibly be forthcoming from the duchess, invitations that could lead to a right bright and busy future.

Carol spent a restless night. Even in her sleep she kept thinking of the hard angry glare in the duke's black eyes and the menacing tone of his deep voice as he had so scathingly bid her goodbye. But, as she promised, she was up early to give Robert his riding lesson and to present him with the gift of her little pet, Imp. As she made her way to the stables, she left Flossie packing her things for the journey home.

This morning she accompanied Robert on his ride. She rode the same horse she rode the day they all went into the village to see the gypsies. For a fleeting moment as she settled herself in the saddle, she thought of the warning the gypsy fortune-teller had given concerning an accident and a tall man. Was there any truth to such a thing? she wondered. She decided not and forced it from her mind as she and Robert cantered out of the courtyard into the gently sloping grounds of the estate. But on their return, she was to think of that warning again, this time with fear and trembling.

Flossie was standing beside Liam at the stable door, dry-washing her hands with her apron, when Lady Carolyn and young Robert came back from their ride. Carol could tell Flossie was quite upset over something, and Liam looked as solemn as a bailiff. Turning Robert over to his groom, she dismounted and went immediately over to where the grim-faced pair stood.

"Whatever's wrong, Flossie? By the look on your faces, I collect something terrible has happened."

"Oh, ma'am!" Flossie said, looking over at Liam, her pert little chin quivering nervously. "Ma'am —ah—that is—ah—" She couldn't seem to get the words out of her mouth.

Liam spoke up then. "Ma'am, there's been an accident. A groom from The Blue Goose Inn just rode in with a message from His Grace. He wants you to come there as soon as possible. He cautioned the groom to be sure and tell you not to say anything to the others in the Castle. He just wants you to come. He doesn't want to alarm the duchess." He swallowed as if just saying the words was a great effort. "Will you go, ma'am?"

An accident—a tall man! The gypsy's warning

buzzed around her head like a gnat. It's come true, she thought. Overton was hurt, maybe dying, and he's calling for me. Even through her distress, that little thought sent a dart of warmth into her chilled soul. "Of course, I'll go, Liam. Will you drive me there?"

She hadn't heard footsteps behind her and was surprised to hear Lord Ravenhill speak quietly as he stepped beside her. "I'll take you, Carol, my carriage is already prepared and ready to go. You and Flossie get in and if we hurry, we can get to The Blue Goose by the noon hour."

"You know about the accident then?" she asked, turning to face him. "Is the groom from the inn still here?"

"Yes, I know about the accident and no, the groom isn't here. I sent him back as soon as he delivered his message." He took her by the elbow, turning her in the direction of his carriage, nodding to Flossie to follow. "Step lively, now, both of you. We don't want to waste any more time."

As soon as both women were settled on one of the seats and Lord Ravenhill was seated opposite them, the coachman pointed the pair of matched grays out of the courtyard and on to the London road. Just before they made the turn from the yard, Carol leaned out the window. "Liam, tell my Aunt what has happened and where I've gone so she won't worry. She can be depended upon to keep the secret from the duchess."

Liam didn't answer, just nodded his head, but Carol assumed he would do her bidding, so she settled back against the squabs, one little worry taken care of. Now she could concentrate on the big worry that enveloped her mind. Her beloved—yes, that's the way she thought of him now—was hurt and calling for her. What if he were dying? What if she didn't reach him in time? Was he calling for her because he loved her or simply because she was the only logical person to come to his aid? Lolly wouldn't know what to do, neither would Cousin Kate. Aunt Minnie would know, but if she had been sent for, the duchess would have become suspicious. No, she was the only dependable person on whom he could call. And yet—and yet—she couldn't really rule out the possibility that he called her out of love. Oh, she hoped that was the reason. She prayed that was the reason. The horses were going as fast as they could safely go, but to her raw nerves it seemed they traveled at a snail's pace. Sitting as taut as a bowstring, she mentally urged the two beasts to strive faster, wishing, like the fabled Pegasus, they could fly.

Lord Ravenhill gave her a gentle smile. "Love is hard to bear, isn't it, Carol? Especially when the object of that love is hurting and you can't bring relief?"

She looked at her cousin, a new respect in her eyes. He knew what she was feeling. No doubt had experienced such a helplessness many times. Oh, not a physical hurting, but a hurting that was just as hard to bear. The hurt that his beloved could never be accepted into the proper society that was destined to be his. And all because the lady he loved was a play-actress. It really wasn't fair.

Love had not dealt fairly with her, either. Because the duke had been hurt by one woman, he's lost trust in all women. Because of her stupidity, she'd lost a chance to prove to him that one unfaithful person did not a world of unfaithful people make. If he lived, she'd tell him so. She'd show him her bitter tongue could be sweet as well. She gripped her hands so tightly, they ached. Oh, hurry, hurry, hurry! Her thoughts raced on with every turn of the wheels.

When she finally reached The Blue Goose Inn she received the shock of her life. The duke wasn't there, had never been there, and there had been no accident.

"What do you make of this, Troy?" she asked, when it finally dawned on her the ostler at the inn was telling the truth.

"Do you suppose Liam got the message garbled and it was at some other inn?" Lord Ravenhill said, not quite meeting her eyes.

"*Blue Goose* doesn't sound like the name of any other inn between Overton Castle and London, and well you know it. I think somebody's bamming us. The question is who?" Carol said, anger beginning to kindle a fire in her amber eyes. "And why?"

"You've had a hard ride, Carol, and anxiety has made you tense. Why don't you go into one of the private parlors and lie down on one of the settles?" Turning to Flossie, who was by now as pale as a ghost, he said, "See if the innkeeper will give you a wet cloth to put on Lady Carolyn's head. It'll made her rest easier."

Flossie mutely agreed, taking off for the kitchen like a scared rabbit. Lord Ravenhill led Carol into one of the parlors, promising to ferret out as much information about all this as he could while she rested. She leaned back against the settle with a long sigh as he closed the door.

After half an hour of trying to lie down under the rough wet cloth Flossie secured, she threw it aside, got up and began to pace the room. Her nerves were strung almost to the breaking point. *Why* had any one sent a message requesting she come to the aid of the Duke of Overton if there'd been no accident? *Who* would do such a thing to her?

As she paced, the small room seemed to grow even smaller, the very walls closing in on her. And she was uncomfortably warm. Leaving in such haste as she did, she still wore the dark blue riding habit she donned to ride with Robert, and underneath the jacket and blouse, her body was damp and sticky with perspiration. Instructing Flossie to remain here in case Lord Ravenhill should return, she decided to go outside. At least, she'd be a bit more comfortable than in this sweltering room, maybe catch a stray breeze or two. Quietly slipping out the parlor door, she made her way towards the back of the inn.

From the taproom, she heard Lord Ravenhill talking to someone, his voice a shade louder than usual. However, she didn't look in, supposing if he found out anything of importance about this wild-goose chase of theirs, he'd come to her. Once outside, she headed for the nearby meadow and the footbridge that spanned the little brook.

The midday sun breathed its fiery breath over all the land, coating every blade of grass, every bush and tree with its white-gold rays. There was no breeze. The willow branches drooped languidly on the grassy banks of the stream and the leaves on the oak trees hung down, too wilted to move. The little brook was the only thing that seemed impervious to the heat. It rippled and gurgled its way over the various rocks that straggled unevenly in its bed. As she did that warm day in early spring, Lady Carolyn sat down on the grassy bank, only this time she didn't remove her boots nor undo her hair. She did, however, remove her jacket and unbutton the collar of her silk blouse as she leaned back against the broad trunk of a sturdy oak, grateful its shady boughs sheltered her from the glaring sun. For the past two nights she had slept very little; then this mysterious message about Overton being in an accident and calling for her and not finding him here when she arrived, all combined to cause a feeling of extreme exhaustion. With her thoughts whirling around like a carousel and the oppressive heat bearing down on her, she grew drowsy. And just as she did on that first fateful day, she wearily closed her eyes and drifted off to sleep.

The sound of a booted foot striking the wooden bridge made her eyes fly open, sleep completely banished. She drew in her breath as she raised her glance to stare into the Duke of Overton's scowling face, his coal-black eyes stabbing her own.

He was the first to speak. With booted feet apart, his black frock-coat pushed back by balled fists implanted on each hip, he said, "You're a bigger fool than I thought, you silly little pea-goose. In the face of all good judgment, you're going to do it, anyway. Well, I won't permit it. I simply will not permit it."

Stunned by his angry blast, Carol slowly got to her feet, her eyes never leaving his stone-cold face.

She drew herself up to her full height, her amber eyes sending fiery darts back into his piercing dark eyes. "Your Grace, I have no idea what you are babbling about, and furthermore, I demand an explanation. Just what is it you will not permit me to do?"

"I will not permit you to elope to Gretna Green to marry that scoundrel Ravenhill. Cousin or no cousin, you will not throw yourself away on such a sterile marriage as he offers."

She was beyond being stunned, she was completely dumbfounded by his words. Finally, finding her voice again, she said, "Gretna Green? Eloping with Troy? Wherever did you get such a notion?"

"I arrived back at the Castle from London less than an hour after you and Ravenhill left. Liam said he thought he heard the words 'elope' and 'Gretna Green,' so he assumed that's where the two of you were heading, stopping here to change horses before heading for the Border. Without ever dismounting, I wheeled my horse around to follow you and stop this foolishness. Thank God, I was in time."

It dawned on her that he must have been the one she heard Troy talking to in the taproom as she made her way out of the inn and towards the meadow. But what did Troy tell him that he believed such a wild tale?

"Have you seen Lord Ravenhill, and if so, what did he say to your accusation?"

"Well, he didn't deny it, neither did he confirm it. He just gave me a disdainful smirk, said it wasn't his place to tell me your plans. He'd let you do that, if you so chose."

A little of the anger went out of his dark eyes, in its place a softer look, a more pleading expression became apparent. He lowered his hands from his hips, letting them hang loosely at his sides. "You can't do this, Carol. You just can't. I threatened Ravenhill with exposure to his family, to the whole of London if necessary, if he insisted on this outrage taking place."

He didn't notice how the use of her pet name slipped out, but Carol did. She also realized who was behind the hoax and why. She just didn't know who was the ringleader—Troy or Liam or Flossie. With the intuition of all females since Eve, she realized something else. The Duke of Overton was in love with her just as she was with him. Only he hadn't discovered it for himself as yet. The fiery anger faded from her eyes, leaving a soft golden glow in its stead. Yet she forced her face to remain cold and stern as she replied. "For your information, I wasn't on my way to Gretna Green to marry Lord Ravenhill, but if I were, what business is it of yours?"

"Because—because—" he looked at her, no longer an arrogant and titled peer of the realm. Now he was just an ordinary man laying his heart at the feet of his chosen maid, "Because—damn it all! You're going to marry me!"

It took all the control she could muster to keep from smiling at him, but he had not yet said the right words.

As she remained silent, struggling for composure, he narrowed his eyes as he looked intently into her still face. "If you weren't on your way to elope with Ravenhill, just why *are* you here? And I want the truth, my lady."

She lowered her eyes, the corners of her mouth twitching the tinest bit. "I, too, had a message from Liam. He said you had hàd an accident here at the inn and were asking for me."

This time it was his turn to be amazed. "Liam told you that? And you came?" That devastating smile of his began to crease his face, his eyes sparkled like bits of jet. "Does that mean what I think it means? You'll accept my offer of marriage?"

Still not smiling and still keeping her eyes lowered, she answered, "It wasn't an offer, it was a demand, an angry demand at that. I see no reason to accept such."

His smile widened. He stepped to where she was standing, went down on one knee, enfolded her right hand in both of his. "If it's a formal declaration you want, Lady Carolyn, you shall have it." Looking up into her eyes, his voice like the tones of a mellow pipe organ, he said, "My dearest one, will you do me the honor of becoming my wife? You have stolen my heart, and I love you beyond all reason."

He had said the right words at last. A lilting giggle escaped from her lips in spite of all she could do, and she returned his smile, her eyes melting into his. Letting go of her hand and rising to his feet, he held out his arms.

"This is where it all began, Carol, my love, only now, like all good fairy tales, let's give ours a happy ending. This time, won't you come into my arms willingly?"

As his strong arms embraced her, she gave a contented little sigh. Resting her head against his broad chest, she said, softly, "I thought you'd never ask."

A deep laugh rumbled in his throat as he held her closer.

Chapter Nineteen

A little discreet cough broke the enchanted moment, and they sprang apart, turning to face a smiling Lord Ravenhill.

"Sorry to intrude on such a tender scene, but there's a little matter of business we have to settle, Your Grace."

For a long minute, the duke and Ravenhill looked at each other. Finally, the duke smiled, held out his hand, saying,

"It looks as if you and I will be in the same family, and since you're no longer a threat to my happiness, I'm willing to bury the hatchet. I'll even forgive you the effrontery of bringing me here," he turned back towards Carol, smiled down into her upturned eyes. "Especially, since it won me such a prize."

Lord Ravenhill inclined his head in a slight bow, the smile still on his face. "I accept your kindness,

Your Grace, but I'm afraid there's more to it than that. I had two accomplices, your groom and Lady Carolyn's abigail. I need to know what you intend to do about them. If they have incurred your disfavor and you intend to dismiss them from service, I'm prepared to give them employment with my staff of servants. What is your pleasure?"

Before the duke had time to reply, Carol spoke up. "Flossie may have overstepped her place a bit, but she did it for me. She brought about the miracle that was needed. I want her to continue to be my abigail."

The Duke gave a lop-sided little grin. "I dislike keeping a groom that showed more sense than I did, but I suppose we all have to make concessions at times. I want Liam to stay, too."

From behind the trunk of a large tree where she had hidden unnoticed, Flossie stepped forward. Rushing to her mistress's side, she grabbed one of Lady Carolyn's hands, bringing it up to her lips and pressing a grateful kiss upon it. "Oh, bless you, ma'am, bless you! I'll never take liberties again, I promise, and I can speak for Liam, too. We're both ever so grateful to you and to you, too, Your Grace."

It was decided that Lord Ravenhill would drive Carol and Flossie back to Overton Castle while the duke, after securing a fresh mount from the inn, would race like the wind to Worster Hall to get Lord Worster's permission to marry his daughter.

Just before mounting into the saddle, the duke turned to Ravenhill. "See that your cousin arrives at the Castle safely, my friend, as I intend to announce our engagement at the *bal masqué* tomorrow night." Quickly darting his eyes over to Carol, he asked, "Does that meet with your approval, my love?"

"Yes, James," Carol said, using his given name for the first time, "that suits me perfectly."

As he rode off in one direction and the carriage pulled out onto the road into another direction, Carol settled back contentedly, never doubting that her father would give his permission to the duke's offer. She choked back a little laugh, though, at the surprise that would surely cover his face when he realized that not only had his daughter captured a dashing and handsome gentleman but the *premier parti* of all England! She couldn't, however, hold back any longer the laugh that bubbled forth as she pictured Aunt Minnie's face when the betrothal was announced at the ball. She would strut and ride the high horse as if she had accomplished it singlehandedly.

Lord Ravenhill gazed over at his laughing cousin. "You sound happy, Carol. You must like the thought of being a duchess."

"Lud! Ma'am, I'd forgotten about that, but 'twill be true. And a grand duchess you'll make, too, I'm thinking," Flossie said, smiling over at her mistress.

A duchess! Truth to tell, she'd forgotten about the title, too. And the power that went along with it. As the coach jogged along the road, her thoughts kept time with the rhythmic clack of the wheels. Liam and Flossie would get married and live happily together at Overton Castle. In time, Lady Laura and Edward would announce their betrothal and subsequent marriage, she felt sure. Already Mr. Lippinscot was happy with his commission in the armed forces. Now all that remained was for Troy and his lady to achieve happiness. And as the Duchess of Overton she could accomplish that, too.

The idea came slowly at first, but the more she thought about it, the more she felt confident it would work. When she went back to Worster Hall to prepare for her wedding, she'd ask for her father's help. She was confident he'd give it, because if Edward were in the same position as Troy, he'd do anything to assure his son's happiness; and thinking almost as much of his nephew as he did his son, he'd help with her devious little plan. Besides, knowing her father as she did, he'd delight in bamming some of London's stiff-necked Society leaders. In a few weeks' time, the French actress Jeanne Dubois would disappear from the London stage and Mrs. Jenny Dinsmore, widow and distant kinswoman, would bring her two-year-old son and take up residence at Worster Hall. Without her dark wigs, no one would connect the two as being the same person, especially when the young Duchess of Overton introduced her to the *ton* at next Season's Assembly. And at the Season's end, when Lord Ravenhill married the young widow and adopted her son as his heir, they, too, could live happily ever afterwards.

Yes, come to think of it, besides winning the love of a man as charming as the duke, she was going to like being a *duchess.*

MASTER NOVELISTS

CHESAPEAKE   CB 24163 $3.95
by James A. Michener

An enthralling historical saga. It gives the account of different generations and races of American families who struggled, invented, endured and triumphed on Maryland's Chesapeake Bay. It is the first work of fiction in ten years to be first on *The New York Times Best Seller List*.

THE BEST PLACE TO BE   PB 04024 $2.50
by Helen Van Slyke

Sheila Callaghan's husband suddenly died, her children are grown, independent and troubled, the men she meets expect an easy kind of woman. Is there a place of comfort? a place for strength against an aching void? A novel for every woman who has ever loved.

ONE FEARFUL YELLOW EYE   GB 14146 $1.95
by John D. MacDonald

Dr. Fortner Geis relinquishes $600,000 to someone that no one knows. Who knows his reasons? There is a history of threats which Travis McGee exposes. But why does the full explanation live behind the eerie yellow eye of a mutilated corpse?

8002

GREAT ROMANTIC NOVELS

SISTERS AND STRANGERS   PB 04445 $2.50
by Helen Van Slyke
     Three women—three sisters each grown into an independent lifestyle—now are three strangers who reunite to find that their intimate feelings and perilous fates are entwined.

THE SUMMER OF THE SPANISH WOMAN
                     CB 23809 $2.50
by Catherine Gaskin
     A young, fervent Irish beauty is alone. The only man she ever loved is lost as is the ancient family estate. She flees to Spain. There she unexpectedly discovers the simmering secrets of her wretched past . . . meets the Spanish Woman . . . and plots revenge.

THE CURSE OF THE KINGS   CB 23284 $1.95
by Victoria Holt
     This is Victoria Holt's most exotic novel! It is a story of romance when Judith marries Tybalt, the young archeologist, and they set out to explore the Pharaohs' tombs on their honeymoon. But the tombs are cursed . . . two archeologists have already died mysteriously.

8000